Torwood's trust

A novel (Vol. 3)

Evelyn Everett-Green

Alpha Editions

This edition published in 2024

ISBN : 9789357968591

Design and Setting By
Alpha Editions
www.alphaedis.com
Email - info@alphaedis.com

Contents

VOL. III.

CHAPTER I.
DETECTED.

YOU have kept your appointment, Monsieur—that is well,' said Mrs. Belassis, in her measured tones. 'I am convinced that we ought to understand one another, that we have the same object in view. It would facilitate matters if you would speak out more frankly, and tell me what is the real object of your visit here.'

'I came to see Mr. Meredith,' answered the Italian, with irritating caution.

Mrs. Belassis would not allow her impatience to betray itself.

'Ostensibly, yes; but you know, and I know, that your real motive was to watch Philip Debenham.'

The stranger smiled significantly.

'To watch the present master of Ladywell—Madame is right.'

'And the motive of this watching is, I presume, not friendship for him?'

The answer did not come so readily as she had expected, and it was still ambiguous.

'Not friendship—not enmity—simple curiosity.'

'Simple curiosity!' repeated Mrs. Belassis; 'that is rather hard to believe. Monsieur, you know you had a deeper motive than that. You have admitted as much on two other occasions. You know that a great injustice is being done.'

'Madame may be right; but on what grounds does she bring so great an accusation against her kinsman?'

'Kinsman!' she echoed wrathfully; 'I claim no kin with him. He is a traitor, a false friend, a treacherous foe. I wash my hands of him altogether. He has behaved villainously to me and mine; I would ruin him gladly if I could, and so would you.'

The Italian looked steadily into her flushed face.

'I am not sure,' he said slowly, 'if I would.'

'You would if you were a man,' she said with some scorn. 'Think of the wrongs your friend is enduring!'

'What friend?'

'Mr. Torwood. Have you forgotten our conversation of only a few days back? You know better than I do what the wrong is; but I know enough.'

'What does Madame know?'

'I know that he is keeping his friend hidden away somewhere, in a kind of captivity (unless he has escaped, as I believe you assured me he had), that he has gained possession of his money and the management of his affairs. I have seen with my own eyes that he is spending Mr. Torwood's money as lavishly as his own. He is behaving scandalously, there can be no doubt whatever of that. If you are a friend of the injured man's, can you not do something to put a stop to it?'

'Why does not Mr. Torwood act for himself?'

'How can I tell? Most likely he cannot. *His friend* has contrived to settle that point satisfactorily. He may be in a madhouse, for aught I know.'

'Madame does not *know* anything, then?'

'No, no facts; but I know quite well that evil is going on, and I mean to check it. Monsieur, will you not help me? If you will but tell me what you know, I will be the one to act; I will relieve you of all the burden of responsibility.'

'What does Madame wish to know?'

'I wish to know where Mr. Torwood is.'

'He is not far away from here.'

'You mean he is in England?'

'Yes, certainly.'

'And near this place?'

'Quite near.'

Mrs. Belassis looked eager and triumphant.

'Monsieur is not jesting?'

'By no means. I do but speak the truth.'

'Can he be at Ladywell—in the village?'

'Madame is right. He is at Ladywell; he has been there for some time.'

Mrs. Belassis stared at him.

'At Ladywell? And I have never seen him!'

The Italian smiled significantly.

'I never said Madame had not seen him.'

Mrs. Belassis began to grow excited.

'Signor Pagliadini, are *you* Mr. Torwood?'

He shook his head, and she looked disappointed.

'I have not that honour.'

'Where, and who is he, then? Monsieur, I entreat you, introduce me to your friend.'

'Madame needs no introduction. Madame is already well acquainted.'

A long silence ensued. Mrs. Belassis' face had grown dark. She seemed half afraid to offer another suggestion.

'You must tell me more, Monsieur.'

But the eager look on the Italian's face had given place to one of hesitation. He looked like a man who has been led on to say more than he at first intended.

'I have said enough,' he answered quickly; 'Madame must not misunderstand me.'

'I begin to think I understand at last.'

Mrs. Belassis spoke very slowly, as if her mind was full of thought—too full to admit of free speech. She pressed her hand to her head, and her eyes seemed to darken and deepen.

'Oh, if *that* is it, what a villain, a scoundrel he has been! But the law will lay a hand upon him. He shall not be allowed to escape.'

'What do you mean?' asked the Italian, who looked somewhat uneasy.

'I mean, Monsieur, that you have let out your secret at last. I know now who and where Mr. Torwood is. Ah! why did I not think of it when Sir Herbert Moncrieff identified him as Torwood—when we all said how utterly unlike any Debenham he was? How could he? How dared he? But he has reached the end of his tether. Now it is my turn.'

The Signor moved restlessly. He looked half interested, half annoyed. He seemed eager, yet reluctant, to speak.

'Madame must be careful and secret. Mr. Torwood is a good friend, but a dangerous enemy.'

Mrs. Belassis pondered over this.

'Where is Mr. Debenham?' she asked suddenly.

'At sea—on a sea-voyage for his health.'

'Does he know of this? Can he have given Mr. Torwood powers to act?'

'He has not done so. He is too ill to know anything about it.'

'Could he not be brought back? He should prosecute at once.'

'Perhaps he would decline to prosecute his friend.'

'Friend!' repeated Mrs. Belassis venomously. Then she added, with an evil look, 'We are Philip Debenham's next-of-kin. *We* will prosecute.'

Her eyes glowed with malicious triumph. She spoke with a relish that was malignant.

'Forgery, fraud, false pretences, gross treachery and wholesale robbery—a very nice list against an English gentleman of honourable name. Yes, Philip Debenham; a little quiet conversation with me will open your eyes considerably. You will not look so bold at the close, as you do at the commencement of our interview.'

But Signor Pagliadini did not seem inclined to allow the matter to slip thus out of his own hands.

'Madame is very confident; but it seems to me that she is too much so. Mr. Torwood is a clever man. Most likely he knows what he is about, and will be quite ready to meet and to fight Madame. Victory is not always to the righteous. It is generally to the strong. Does not your proverb say that possession is nine points of the law?'

'You mean he would dispute the possession?'

Mrs. Belassis seemed to pause and reflect. That was a new and unwelcome idea. She even wondered if the Italian could by any chance have tried to put her upon a wrong tack, for he was anything but open with her.

Torrington Torwood—Philip Debenham; the names seemed to float as in a mist before her, and she could not disentangle the one from the other. She was convinced one moment that the present master of Ladywell *must* be Philip Debenham—he could not otherwise assume such mastery; and surely no one else would dare to play the part he was playing: it would be too reckless, too dangerous. And yet a host of small doubts and suspicions crowded upon her, one after the other, all pointing to the strange conclusion that the man was an impostor, not Philip Debenham at all, but merely someone who understood his affairs as well as he did himself—in other words, Torrington Torwood.

Mrs. Belassis' head seemed fairly to swim. If only the Italian would speak out and ratify in actual words the hints he had thrown out. His manner was so odd that she found herself inclined to doubt even such statements as he had made. What if he were an enemy too, leading her on to worse troubles than already beset her path?

Mrs. Belassis was thoroughly uncomfortable, devoured by curiosity and uncertainty, yet too distrustful of her companion to press him with further inquiries.

She made one last attempt to draw him out.

'Whether or not he is the right man, I am convinced that he will retain the place he has gained, be it by fair means or foul. He has strength, wealth, determination, and this three months has enabled him to settle himself firmly in possession. Philip Debenham had better look to himself when he returns from sea. This man has all the property, and will take care that he keeps it. He will dispute the possession by every weapon in his power, and he will win.'

The Signor looked uneasy.

'You think that?'

'I am convinced of it. I have studied his character closely. He is proud, and he is unscrupulous. He will never submit to be humiliated. He will fight to the death. It is might, not right, that conquers in such a struggle, and he has the power.'

Signor Pagliadini looked irresolute, like a man who half wishes, half fears to speak.

'Then you would not prosecute?'

'I should have to think seriously before I did so. My husband would be swayed in the matter by me. If we were absolutely convinced of our cause, we might be inclined to do so; much would depend upon the character and appearance of Philip Debenham when he appeared. We could not act unless the whole case were frankly confided to us.'

She paused, but the Italian did not seem inclined to speak, so she added impressively:

'If you are concerned in this matter, Monsieur, and have the interests of your friend really at heart, you cannot do better than confide in me. I am anxious that justice should be done; but I cannot act in the dark. Have you nothing more to tell me?'

There was a little hesitation before the answer came; but it was quite decided then.

'No, Madame; nothing more, I thank you.'

'I hope you may not regret your decision when it is too late,' said Mrs. Belassis loftily, as she rose and turned away. 'Good-morning, Monsieur.'

Mrs. Belassis walked home in a state of mind bordering on distraction. She would have given anything in the world to have been absolutely certain that this supposed nephew of hers was an impostor. She hated him so cordially, that no trouble would be too great to compass his ruin, if only she could be sure of her position.

She had many grounds of suspicion; many incidents rose to her mind, all pointing to the desired conclusion, and the Italian had certainly told her that Torwood was at Ladywell, and Philip Debenham at sea. But then came maddening doubts of the stranger's truthfulness; and it would be too humiliating to set on foot a charge which could not be substantiated, especially such a serious one as this.

She reached home in a restless and perturbed state, and found that a cloud seemed to hang over the atmosphere of Thornton House. Bertha was pouting and kicking the leg of her chair, and Matilda's eyes looked as if they had been shedding tears. Her face was angry and discontented.

'Is anything the matter?' asked Mrs. Belassis, as she took her seat at the luncheon-table.

Neither her husband nor her son were present, and the three ladies had the room to themselves.

'Nothing particular. I don't suppose you will care. You never do care for our interests, Matilda's or mine. Only Phil's engaged to be married.'

'Philip engaged! To whom, pray?'

'To Roma Meredith, of all people in the world! We met old Mr. Meredith out driving, and he told us. It is a shame! There's nothing whatever in her to make him care for her. It's only because she's had such chances.'

Mrs. Belassis made no reply. She fancied she might make capital out of what she had just heard. She was convinced that the Italian was in love with Roma, and jealousy is a powerful incentive to revenge.

'It is too bad!' cried Matilda, with a half-sob. 'And Phil was so nice and kind and attentive when he first came, and was always quite friendly until people made it so horrid for him that he couldn't come any more. I do call it too bad!'

'So do I,' rejoined Bertha. 'It's a great shame. I'm sure we had as good a chance as anyone, until mamma spoilt it by being so disagreeable to him.'

Anger and disappointment robbed the two girls of their customary dread of their mother.

'The best match in the county,' grumbled Matilda. 'And we might have taken our chance with anyone, if we'd only had fair play.'

'Mamma, how can you sit there smiling in that aggravating way?' burst out Bertha spitefully. 'You know it's your fault. You've always set yourself against our interests. I call it dreadful for anyone's mother to be so unkind. And now you don't seem to care one bit!'

'What should I care about, pray? Do be more explicit and less violent.'

Bertha turned away angrily.

Matilda answered sulkily enough:

'One of us might have married him, if we'd had a fair chance.'

'A good thing for you you have not; he is no fit match for one of my daughters.'

'Mamma! What do you mean?'

'I mean that I shall look higher for you than that—cousin of yours.'

'Mamma! He is master of Ladywell!'

'*Is* he master of Ladywell?' responded Mrs. Belassis, with more spitefulness than caution. 'That remains to be proved.'

'Mamma! What do you mean?'

'That I hardly know. I have been hearing a very curious story to-day.'

'Oh, what? Do tell us? About Phil?'

'Well, to speak more accurately, I should say about the man we have called Phil all this time.'

Bertha's eyes were bright with excitement.

'Oh, then there is a mystery after all! I always did think there was something odd about Phil, ever since Sir Herbert Moncrieff was so surprised that he was Mr. Debenham, not Mr. Torwood.'

Mrs. Belassis looked at her.

'You suspected something odd then?'

'Yes; what Sir Herbert said afterwards, when he saw Maud, was so funny. I didn't mean to tell anyone, and I promised Phil I wouldn't; but if he's going to marry Roma, I don't care about keeping his secret any longer.'

'Speak out, child. What secret? Did he confide in you, and ask you to keep quiet? Just explain yourself,' said Mrs. Belassis impatiently.

'I will, if you'll only give me time.'

Bertha, who liked to be important, was delighted to be able to impart anything so interesting to her mother.

'You heard how Sir Herbert greeted Phil as Mr. Torwood, and how surprised he was when Phil told him his name was Debenham?'

'Yes, yes; go on.'

'Well, when we were walking about the gardens together, and he saw Maud, he knew directly who she was, because he said she was so exactly like the Philip Debenham he had met in America. When he remembered that Tor had just said *he* was Philip Debenham he got a little confused, and evidently didn't quite know what to say. However, I didn't pretend to notice particularly what he had said, and we dropped the subject. But I didn't forget it, and I told Phil about it one day soon afterwards.'

'Did you? What did he say? Was he put out?' asked Mrs. Belassis eagerly.

'No, not at all; at least, he didn't seem so. He didn't seem to care a bit; and he laughed when I promised to say nothing about it, and didn't appear to mind at all. He made me think very little of it myself.'

'That was his cunning,' said Mrs. Belassis viciously. 'It is quite in keeping with his cool audacity and daring all throughout. Bertha, your evidence is of the greatest value at such a juncture. It is proof positive of the suspicion I have been puzzling over for an hour or more.'

'Oh! what, mamma? Do tell us!' urged Matilda.

'I believe I know!' cried Bertha, whose wits were the quickest. 'Phil is not Phil at all, but Mr. Torwood; and he has been pretending all the while to be Phil. Isn't that it, mamma?'

'That is what I strongly suspect,' said Mrs. Belassis, with more of her usual deliberation; 'but girls, no word of this is to be breathed until I give you leave. A gross wrong has been committed, and a heartless fraud perpetrated. We, as Philip Debenham's next-of-kin, cannot suffer things to go on unexposed and unpunished; but we shall defeat our own ends if we go to work rashly, or show our hand too soon. You must be silent as the grave until the time comes for the exposure.'

The girls looked excited.

'But what will happen, mamma? Will Phil be sent to prison?'

'I should hope so. I should expect a heavy sentence for so deliberate and treacherous a crime. The penalty for forgery is a heavy one.'

A few days—nay, a few hours back, Matilda and Bertha would have been filled with compassion for the unhappy criminal. Now, however, their feelings had undergone a revolution, and their interest in him had dwindled to a mere shadow. The excitement of a crime and prosecution far outweighed any feeling of commiseration for the victim.

'Oh, mamma, how dreadful! Will there be a trial? Shall we have to be witnesses? What will Phil look like? Oh, how wicked he must be!'

'And then there will be another Phil to come here!' cried Matilda, with animation. 'Another Phil ten times as nice as this one, I dare say. I wonder what he will be like, and what he will say to it all. Mamma, where is the real Phil? Why didn't he come? Why did he let Mr. Torwood go on so?'

'I believe he has been very ill, and entirely in Mr. Torwood's power. I do not yet know exactly where he is, or what is the matter with him; but I shall find out all in due time, no doubt. It is evident that he has not been a free agent during this crisis; and now he has been sent on a sea-voyage to get him still farther out of the way, whilst Mr. Torwood strengthens himself more and more in his position. I shall make every effort to find Philip, and bring him over here. When we once have the true heir in our keeping, the false one must abdicate. Maud's likeness to her brother will prove of inestimable value.'

'And Maud is so fond of that dreadful Mr. Torwood,' said Matilda. 'Whatever *will* she say!'

'It has been the most disgraceful affair from first to last,' said Mrs. Belassis, with righteous indignation; 'but it shall soon be brought to an ignominious conclusion.'

'And Phil, the real Phil, will be so fond of us!' cried Bertha eagerly. 'He will be so grateful to mamma—and to me too—for having found it all out; and to papa and mamma for bringing him back, and helping him against that wicked man he thought was his friend! Oh, it will all be so different and so nice! There will be no more quarrels now. Phil will quite seem to belong to us; and I'm sure he will always feel that he can never be grateful enough, or do enough for us, for doing so much for him. It will be altogether delightful!'

This was an eminently pleasing view of the matter, and the sisters became enthusiastic.

'Oh, mamma, how long will it be before something happens? Please tell us what you are going to do!'

'My first step,' said Mrs. Belassis deliberately, 'will be to have an interview with this man who calls himself Philip Debenham. After that, I shall know better on what ground we stand.'

CHAPTER II.
THE ATTACK.

HAVE you ever examined the securities of Maud's trust-money?' asked Miss Marjory of Tor. 'Do you know how it is invested, or what interest has been accumulating? The interest, even of the five thousand only, will have mounted up in eighteen years. Have you ever made inquiries into the question?'

'I have made a few inquiries; but I have not elicited much information. Mr. Belassis—as guardian, trustee, and executor—has had full power over the money all this time, and has seen fit to resent any kind of questioning from me.'

'That looks bad,' said Miss Marjory. 'That man is a rogue, Philip.'

'I am aware of it.'

'A pretty sort of trustee! How could Mr. Debenham have trusted him?'

'I believe he did not do so. I believe he made a later will. I believe this one was a mere blind——'

'A later will!' cried Miss Marjory exultantly. 'Why, of course he did—that would explain it all. I could not conceive how a sane man——But where *is* the later will, then? Why is it not produced? Why does this one stand?'

Tor shook his head.

'We are afraid it fell into the hands of Belassis, as the mass of papers did. You know as well as I, what its fate would be then.'

'You think he has destroyed it?'

'I do.'

Miss Marjory paused, with her head on one side. By-and-by she said:

'So do not I.'

'Why not?'

'Because he is so unequivocally anxious for Maud's marriage with his son. Maud would only bring in a dowry of five thousand, as matters stand now— a mere pittance for a young lady of refined and expensive tastes. But if he suspects the existence of a later will, his anxiety is explained. When Maud is his son's wife, he could snap his fingers at any discovery.'

Tor's eyes brightened.

'There is a great deal in what you say, Miss Marjory. I have not been blind to the strangeness of Mr. Belassis' eagerness for the marriage. I taxed him with it once, and asked point-blank for his motive. You may guess whether he told it.'

'We must find that will!' cried Miss Marjory, with energy. 'It must be hidden away somewhere. But where can it be?'

'I am much afraid it must have perished. The house Mr. Debenham lived in has been pulled down and rebuilt, and the furniture sold. You may be sure Belassis would have made an exhaustive search, if his suspicions had been excited, as is likely enough.'

'If his were not, his wife's would be,' said Miss Marjory decidedly. 'Those two Belassis', husband and wife, are as big a pair of knaves as ever walked the earth.'

The door opened, and the servant announced: 'Mrs. Belassis.'

'Talk of——' began Miss Marjory.

'Show her in,' said Tor aloud; adding, in a low voice, 'What can she have come for?'

'Mischief,' answered Miss Marjory, her eyes sparkling. 'May I stay?'

'By all means.'

'If she is too disagreeable. I shall put in my word. I can silence her if needful.'

There was no time for more, for Mrs. Belassis was at the door.

Tor rose to receive her; but his greeting was somewhat cold. After their last passage-at-arms, Mrs. Belassis had not disguised her unfriendly feelings.

Miss Marjory merely bowed slightly; and the keen brightness and alertness of her gaze did not altogether please the visitor.

'I have come to see you on business,' said she, as she seated herself and looked at Tor.

'I shall be happy to give your business all possible consideration,' he answered politely.

'It is not *my* business,' said Mrs. Belassis, with significance. 'But it is of a private nature;' and here she looked at Miss Marjory, who did not stir.

'Does the privacy of its nature concern you or me?' questioned Tor.

'You, of course. Do you imagine I should discuss my private affairs with *you*?'

'And yet,' remarked Tor, with a smile, 'you expect me, it would seem, to discuss my private affairs with you.'

'I shall give you no option,' said Mrs. Belassis, with acrimony; 'but remember they are private.'

Again she looked at Miss Marjory, who merely smiled, not altogether without malice.

'I have a taste for dabbling in other people's private affairs,' she said audaciously. 'I think you would be surprised if you knew some of the things I know about the lives of people almost unknown to me.'

Mrs. Belassis made no reply, but felt vaguely uneasy. Tor said quietly:

'Miss Marjory Descartes is my very good friend. If what you have to say relates only to me and my affairs, she is welcome to hear it.'

'Oh, very well,' answered Mrs. Belassis viciously. 'If you have no sense of shame yourself, I'm sure I do not wish to spare you. All the world may know what I know, for aught I care. Indeed, they soon will do, and you will see then how far your precious popularity will carry you. You will find yourself in a felon's dock before the next assize is over, if you do not play a very different game from the one you are doing now.'

Tor listened with a coolness which was a little disconcerting to the excited woman before him. Forewarned was forearmed in his case, and he evinced nothing but an amused incredulity in face or voice.

'Indeed! this is most interesting. I had no idea such greatness loomed before me. Pray go on; it is like a chapter from Wilkie Collins. Isn't it exciting, Miss Marjory?'

'Very. It always amuses me to see people make egregious blunders,' answered Miss Marjory affably. 'I hope Mrs. Belassis has a great deal more to tell us.'

Mrs. Belassis felt her face grow pale with rage. She had never before had any statement of hers treated with anything so like ridicule.

'I have a good deal more to tell you,' she answered, with suppressed savageness; 'and you may thank me for great consideration that you hear it first through me, and not through a lawyer.'

'I am ready to thank you even for a fancied consideration,' answered Tor quietly; 'but let me tell you that I would much rather hear anything you may have to say from a lawyer than from you. I know how to deal with a man, and with a libel; but to a lady and a relative, and in my own house, it is difficult to find any suitable reply to whatever charges she may see fit to bring.'

'I am not a relative; and you are not in your own house—you know that as well as I.'

Miss Marjory lifted her eyebrows, shrugged her shoulders, and smiled a smile that was truly exasperating, as she glanced at Tor. The look said as plainly as words could do, 'Is she mad?'

Mrs. Belassis, strong though she felt her cause, began to wish she had waited for a few proofs before making an attack. The ground under her feet was not secure enough to warrant an encounter with two such foes as she now saw before her.

'I am quite ready to repudiate our relationship, now that I find it is as unwelcome to you as it is to me,' said Tor coolly; 'but I repeat once more, that in my own house I cannot answer in fitting terms a lady who chooses to insult me. If it is all the same to you, Mrs. Belassis, I would rather you let me hear whatever you have to say through your husband, or through a lawyer. If you have any charge to bring against me, as your words seem to imply, you had better have your case made out in the usual way.'

Mrs. Belassis knew that as matters stood at present she had no case; and the cool scorn of her adversary's tone stung her to the quick. She *knew* he was an impostor, yet she had no real evidence to bring forward. But she was not going to be silenced so easily.

'I shall act as I choose, and speak as I choose, and when I choose,' she answered angrily. 'Bold and wicked as you are, I have my hand on the clue which will in the end bring shame and ruin upon you. Where is *your friend*, Torrington Torwood?'

'At sea, on a voyage for his health.'

'He is not. He is in England. He is at Ladywell. He is in this very house?'

'Indeed! If you are so well informed as to my friend's movements, why come to me?'

'Your friend!' she echoed scornfully; 'friend, indeed! Why do you even try to keep up the deception when all is known? You are Torrington Torwood yourself!'

'How very interesting! Well, I have played the part often enough to feel quite at home in it. Produce your "Philip Debenham," and I will gladly abdicate in his favour. It will not be the first time we have changed names and situations.'

Mrs. Belassis grew more and more excited. It is very aggravating when we know we have got hold of the truth, not to have power to make it recognised and admitted by others.

'Do you mean to say that you are prepared to *swear*,' she began, with great emphasis—'to swear that you are Philip Debenham?'

'I am prepared to swear a good deal in the right place and at the right time,' answered Tor, with a steady look at Mrs. Belassis out of his great grey eyes, which was not agreeable to her. 'But to you I shall certainly decline to swear anything at all. You have thought fit to accuse and insult me in my own house, being fully aware that under the circumstances you could do so with impunity. You have, however, reached the extreme limit; and for your own sake I should advise you to be content with the answers you have already received. As I have said before, if you have any charge against me, you had better send it through the right channel—that of the law.'

Miss Marjory nodded her head approvingly; she admired Tor's high-handed way of carrying things, and could see that it quite took his enemy by surprise, and disquieted her somewhat; at the same time, she thought a little more diplomatic questioning would have been advisable before a declaration of open defiance had been made. They were quite ignorant as to the strength of the adversary's cause, and it was hardly politic, perhaps, to court the intervention of the law, although it was probably, in the present position of affairs, something of an idle threat.

She was not altogether sorry that at this crisis of the conversation, Tor was called suddenly away. He was not sorry, neither was Mrs. Belassis, for the interruption. She had no intention of leaving without another attempt to elicit the truth, bringing forward at the same time her evidence, such as it was, which would most likely produce some effect; and she was glad of a pause, which would enable her to think over what she meant to say.

Miss Marjory, however, did not leave her long in peace. The door had hardly closed behind Tor before she began briskly:

'Really, Mrs. Belassis, I am intensely interested in all you say. It is quite like a romance, this doubt you have cast upon my friend's identity. Do tell me some more. What can have made you think such a thing?'

'Everybody can see that this man is not a Debenham, and people who met him abroad all know him as Torwood. Signor Pagliadini, though not willing to take an active share in the accusation, knows perfectly well that this man is Torwood, and that Philip Debenham is at sea. And, moreover, the real Philip Debenham is strikingly like Maud, who has, as you see, no resemblance at all to this impostor.'

'Really, how very interesting! You surprise me. That point about the likeness is very remarkable. You are perhaps aware that I was intimately acquainted with Mr. Torwood's father; and when I happened to see a photograph of Mr. Debenham's friend, I was much struck by the very strong likeness it bore to

Guy Torwood, whom I once knew so well. Curious how likenesses strike different persons, is it not? Signor Pagliadini thinks him like Maud. I think him like my old friend. Odd, is it not? There is no accounting for such things.'

Mrs. Belassis looked floored. Miss Marjory spoke so easily and naturally that it was hard to imagine she was playing a part; yet, if what she said was true, one great fraction of her evidence was all but demolished.

'You knew—Mr. Torwood's father,' she stammered. 'And the photograph this—this man showed you, as Mr. Torwood's, was like his father?'

'Strikingly so. I recognised it at once from its likeness. I must see now if I can trace in it any likeness to Maud.'

'Sir Herbert Moncrieff, who met Maud at a party, was much struck by it; and he called this Philip Debenham, Torwood,' said Mrs. Belassis.

Miss Marjory seemed to consider.

'Well, Mrs. Belassis, the whole question seems rather a puzzling one; but I cannot think it likely, from what I know of our friend, that he would run his head into a noose for nothing. In all probability things are as he says; but, if not, you may be quite sure he is acting as his friend's agent, with his friend's consent—probably at his request. Those two men have been devoted friends for eighteen years—is it likely one would suddenly take a mania—for robbing and defrauding the other? Whatever is being done is, you may be certain, done by mutual agreement; and you would find yourself in a very awkward position if you took my young friend's hint, and went to law, only to find yourself the laughing-stock of the nephew, whose cause you thought you were promoting. I believe, too, that no one could prosecute but the injured party. I leave you to judge whether this is probable.'

But Mrs. Belassis, though somewhat taken aback, was not to be so easily suppressed.

'My nephew is ill, and unable to act for himself. I have reason to believe that his mind is temporarily affected. He is quite in his friend's power, and most unscrupulous use is being made of this power. We, as next-of-kin, are bound to protect him, and we will do so at all risk. Let Torrington Torwood look to himself!' the last words were added with such animus that Miss Marjory's lip curled.

'You are very generous, certainly, towards this mythical nephew of yours, whose existence you have presupposed. Do you not think you are actuated in reality by your curious and incomprehensible dislike to—my Mr. Debenham? If so, you may soon find yourself in a very awkward position.'

'Incomprehensible!' echoed Mrs. Belassis. 'He has done nothing but insult and oppose us ever since he came back. He has a smooth tongue, but he is our enemy at heart, and he will do us an ill-turn when he can. He knows that, and I believe you know it too.'

'I do not know it. What I do know is that he has been wonderfully considerate towards you; and although he is acquainted with facts which must seriously affect your peace of mind, and might bring you the greatest unhappiness a woman can suffer, he has refrained from letting fall one syllable which could injure you, in spite of all the provocation you have given him. I advise you, however, not to go too far. A man's patience is not supposed to be a very elastic article. If you do not take care, you may find the tables turned upon yourself.'

Mrs. Belassis looked uneasy.

'What can you know about my affairs? Has this Philip, as he calls himself, told you more than he tells me?'

'Perhaps he has; but in this instance it was I who told him.'

'What did you tell him?'

Miss Marjory looked at her without answering.

'What did you tell him?' repeated Mrs. Belassis.

'Do you really wish to know? It will not be pleasant news.'

'I do wish to know.'

'I suppose you are not aware that your husband was married in 1843?'

'Married!' gasped Mrs. Belassis.

'Married, in Whitbury Minster, to a girl named Nelly Roberts, who had been in my service as lady's-maid. He deserted her two months after the marriage, and, so far as I know, never heard of her again.'

Mrs. Belassis sat like one turned to stone.

'What became of her?' she asked, when she could find voice.

'She lived for some time in Whitbury, and then her health failed, and she went away. Eventually she died; but I lost sight of her before then.'

'When did she die?'

'Not long after February, 1850; but I do not know the exact date.'

'I was married in the May of that year,' said Mrs. Belassis.

'I know; and I hope—I hope—at any rate, inquiries are being made, and we shall soon learn the truth; but I do not for a moment believe your husband knows anything about the matter. I believe he lost sight of her utterly.'

Mrs. Belassis said nothing for awhile. Then she asked:

'My nephew knows this?'

'He does.'

'Why did he not tell me?'

'I believe he wished to spare you.'

'Then why do you tell me now?'

'Because I wish to warn you. It seems to me that you are taking a very unwise course; and I think it fair you should know to what it may lead you, if you too far provoke your nephew.'

Mrs. Belassis, however, was not long subdued. Her heart certainly misgave her; but she would not show it; and she had a lingering hope that perhaps Belassis did know more of the history of his first wife than Miss Marjory supposed. She had no great opinion of his moral character or ability; but she doubted whether he would dare to commit a crime like bigamy.

'I shall do as I think right,' she said, with a loftiness of manner which was well assumed, though only an assumption. 'Justice must be done, at all costs. I may have been wronged, but I will not permit wrong to go unpunished.'

Vials of wrath were being stored up to be poured upon the head of Belassis; but here matters must be carried with a high hand.

'Please yourself,' answered Miss Marjory pleasantly. 'You seem to me very anxious to court defeat and ridicule, but that is certainly your business, not mine.'

Mrs. Belassis felt that the interview had lasted long enough, and she rose to go.

'Mr. Torwood does not seem inclined to hurry back,' she said, 'so I will not intrude upon you longer. Tell him, with my compliments, that if he declines to listen to me, he will soon be forced to listen to Signor Pagliadini.'

Mrs. Belassis walked rapidly from the house, her mind in a tumult of angry feeling and horrible uneasiness as regards her own position. So engrossed was she, that she did not perceive, until close upon him, the Italian, who was walking up to Ladywell to pay the promised visit. When face to face, she stopped short and said:

'They will dispute it. He means to keep the name and position he has assumed. Try your power, if you will; but his mind is made up.'

Then, without waiting for a reply, she resumed her rapid pace.

Signor Pagliadini was strangely preoccupied that first evening at Ladywell. Make what effort he would, it was plain to all that he had something on his mind. It did not, then, surprise Tor overmuch when, as the household was preparing to disperse that night, he said:

'Can I speak with you a few moments in private?'

'Certainly, Signor,' said Tor readily.

'I am anxious not to be interrupted,' continued the Italian, with something of nervous constraint in his manner. 'Would it be asking too much that you should join me in my room, when your leisure permits it?'

'I will be with you in ten minutes,' said Tor. 'I have to go round the house, as usual. I will not keep you waiting long.'

'Do not hurry, Signor,' said the Italian courteously. 'I will await your convenience.'

He went upstairs with his candle.

'It is coming now,' said Tor to Miss Marjory, as he handed her hers. 'Whatever it is, I shall hear it now.'

'Put on a bold face, then,' advised Miss Marjory, 'as you did this afternoon. Never say die! You will pull through yet.'

'Perhaps; but something tells me that this man is a very different kind of adversary from Mrs. Belassis.'

Miss Marjory was privately of the same opinion, but she would not betray her uneasiness.

'I wish I could be present to support you again, but that would hardly do. Be bold, and admit nothing. You have my best wishes; and come what may, I will stand by you.'

'I believe it, and am grateful,' said Tor; and then they shook hands warmly, and after the nightly prowl round the house, Tor, with rather a sinking heart, mounted to Signor Pagliadini's room.

CHAPTER III.
A STRANGE AWAKENING.

IT will be necessary now to make a break in the continuity of the story, and return to the spotless bedchamber in Dr. Schneeberger's house, where the real Phil Debenham lay so long.

For many weeks after Tor had left him, he remained in a state of helpless torpor—knowing nothing, hearing nothing, seeing nothing—merely taking what nourishment was given in a mechanical fashion, from which all power of volition seemed absent.

But gradually a change came over the sick man. By slow degrees, and without any visible alteration in his condition, his brain began to recover its faculties, and long before he was inclined to evince any sign of life, he was able to hear, and in part to comprehend, what went on around him.

At first his thoughts were very dim and indistinct, and he was chiefly disturbed by a haunting dread that Tor had left him. He missed him, in a blind, unreasoning way, and was vaguely distressed by the absence of his friend, before he had really realized that he was alone.

As his brain-power gradually strengthened he took in other things.

He found that, to this unknown household, wherever it might be, he was known as Herr Torwood, and over this strange metamorphosis he puzzled long and helplessly, and threw himself again into unconsciousness for some days.

When he woke again, his mind was still clearer. He gave, however, no sign of comprehension, partly because the effort to awake his benumbed faculties seemed greater than he cared as yet to make, partly because a vague mistrust and uneasiness had fallen upon him, and he felt that he must gain a clearer insight into his surroundings, before he allowed it to be seen that he had come to himself.

One day, whilst he was in this state, the little German, whom he supposed to be a doctor, because of his daily visits and careful examinations—one day this German doctor brought with him a medical friend, to whom he talked long and learnedly over the supposed condition of his patient's brain.

Doctors and Germans, however, are not above gossip, and after the medical side of the subject had been exhaustively discussed, they fell into another vein.

'The Herr Debenham, his rich friend, will be very much disturbed at this long insensibility,' remarked Dr. Schneeberger.

'Where, then, is this Herr Debenham? Does he visit his friend often?'

'No, he cannot. He is in England. I think he is a great lord there. He has come into some very vast property, I believe. Gretchen thinks so, from what he told her when he was here, after he had brought his friend to us. His letters come from a Ladywell Manor. I believe an English Manor is equal to a Schloss with us. He may be a Graf, for all I know.'

'He pays well for his friend here, I suppose?'

'Very well. He is a true Englishman for that. He was so anxious to leave Herr Torwood with me, that I believe he would have paid any sum I chose to ask. Ah! yes; he is a liberal patron. I have a great respect for Herr Debenham. Such a handsome Englishman, too!'

'Well to be his friend, then,' said the other. 'Does he purpose to come and see this one ever?'

'I am to send for him the moment I detect any sign of returning sensibility. He is very anxious to be with his friend when he awakes from this long sleep. I confess I, too, am anxious that he should be here, in case what he expects should take place.'

'What does he expect?'

'He tells me that upon a former occasion, when the Herr Torwood became unconscious for a short time, he came to himself, believing himself to be Herr Debenham; and it was a good while before he could be convinced of his own identity. Now this is a very curious symptom, and will be interesting to watch; but as I am a stranger to Herr Torwood, I would rather his own friend was with him to convince him of his error. I might find it difficult.'

'What an odd thing!' said the second doctor. 'I never heard of a similar case. I wonder if it will be so?'

'Herr Debenham, I am sure, anticipates it. He has alluded to it more than once in his letters. He tells me that they have, from time to time, passed under each other's names during their travels, which may perhaps account, to a certain extent, for the confusion of ideas.'

'Perhaps; still, it is an odd symptom. One would be curious to watch its development.'

And then the two doctors took their departure, leaving the patient, they supposed to be so utterly vacant, in a very perturbed state.

Phil's mind was not altogether clear, the true balance of his faculties was not entirely restored. He could understand a great deal, but he could not weigh possibilities, or grasp a complex situation, as he could have done at another time.

Had he been able to do this, it is probable he might have guessed somewhat at Tor's motive for acting as he had done. His entire confidence in his friend would have sustained him until he could see him face to face, and learn the truth from his own lips. But in its present clouded state, his mind could only take in one thing at a time; and the fact which he had firmly grasped, through overhearing this conversation, was that his friend had defrauded him of his name and position, and was living upon his estate, whilst he had taken care that the real possessor should not be believed when he did recover consciousness, and have power to assert his claim.

Ladywell was a name well known to Phil. The Manor House had been his ideal of all a house should be, from his childhood's days, when he and little Maud had played in secluded corners of the park. The old uncle, who was regarded as something of an ogre, to be feared and avoided, was only dimly remembered; but Phil had always known that he was his great-uncle's natural heir, and with the buoyant hopefulness of his nature, had entertained a dim expectation that the property might, by some lucky chance, come to him, either by testamentary bequest, or (in absence of will) as heir-at-law.

Evidently this is what had taken place. The old man had died. The property had come to him, and Tor, forgetting under pressure of temptation all his old honour and uprightness, had taken advantage of Phil's helplessness, and of the fact that he was a perfect stranger to his own relations, and had claimed the inheritance as his own, calmly transferring his own name and personality to his unconscious friend, and adopting Phil's instead.

Phil writhed in helpless irritation and dismay when the whole force of the situation broke upon him. He had no clue to Tor's real motive; naturally it did not occur to him to imagine it. He could think of nothing but the treacherous way in which he had been defrauded, and of what possible steps he could take to free himself from the net which had been cast about him.

One thing was self-evident. He must remain in a state of apparent insensibility for the present. If he betrayed one gleam of consciousness, Tor would be summoned; and once let Tor's strong hand close over him, and Phil knew that he should be powerless. He had not lived eighteen years in close company, without knowing Tor's strength of will and purpose; and he knew that in an open struggle he would simply be crushed. Tor's word, not his, would be believed; and if he were to be resolute in his declaration that he was Philip Debenham, he might, for all he knew, be housed in a madhouse before many days were over.

It was a terrible suspicion, and quite sufficed to keep up all Phil's determination to remain quiet until he had matured some plan of escape.

From time to time some of the old loving confidence in Tor would assert itself, and Phil would be half tempted to have him summoned, and learn from his own lips how it was that he had acted thus; but then again doubts and fears filled his mind, and the risk seemed too great a one to run.

Suppose Tor was his enemy? Suppose, having made one false step, he had then advanced until retreat should be impossible? Such things had happened before, and might happen again. When once a man had fallen, had begun a course of deceit and treachery, it was a hard matter to draw back. Phil was ready to believe that Tor might have acted, in the first place, simply from an impulse of ambition; but he could not get over his fear, that having once announced to the world that he was Philip Debenham, and assumed the position at Ladywell Manor to which the name entitled him, he would be prepared to stick to his colours at all cost, and would never admit himself a liar, an impostor, and a forger.

No; come what might, Tor would make up his mind, and he would yield to nothing but actual force. He would never submit to humiliation and disgrace, and he had evidently taken every means in his power to ensure himself against danger. He would never willingly let Phil escape from his clutches, and therefore it would be necessary to use subtlety before he could hope to obtain his freedom.

For many days Phil lay silent and motionless, making plans and weighing possibilities. As the helplessness of his condition grew more and more apparent, so did his bitterness increase against his former friend.

'Friend' indeed! Phil often smiled mournfully over the mockery of the word; and would lie for hours brooding over the strange, mysterious change which must have come over Tor, before he could stoop to such treachery and baseness. 'Mine own familiar friend,' he would sometimes murmur to himself over and over again; 'mine own familiar friend,' until the words seemed to haunt him night and day, as the most expressive in the whole language of thought. Yes, it was ever so; it was no new thing, this sudden betrayal of confidence, this treacherous attack from one who had answered to the sacred name of friend. It had been true thousands of years ago, and it was true that day. The history of the world could furnish countless instances of that same crime; and as the great Roman Emperor found, it was the hand of the familiar friend which was readiest to strike the deathblow.

'Et tu, Brute?'

Those words of dignity and pathos have passed into a household word, but never before had Phil so realized their melancholy and touching significance.

'Mine own familiar friend'—yes, indeed. It was to that very familiarity, that implicit confidence which existed between them that Tor owed the power to practise this great deception. This was an added pang, and cost Phil many hours of bitter thought.

He had learned during these days of consciousness how this household, of which he seemed a member, divided its time. He knew when food would be brought up for him, and at what hour the doctor paid his daily visit. He knew when to expect the maid to sweep out the room and dust the furniture, and he equally knew when he should be left long hours in solitude.

One day, at this time, he tried the experiment of getting up. He found his strength less impaired than he had feared, for he had but a dim idea of the flight of time, and did not know if months or weeks had passed since he had been laid low, nor did he understand exactly what it was that had ailed him.

After a few trials, made day by day, he was able to stand and walk without any great difficulty; the giddiness he experienced at first diminished with every trial.

Soon he was able to stand and sit for some time; and he then began a careful search for any papers which Tor might have left behind, by accident or design, which could throw any light upon the subject which so haunted him.

He soon saw that an exchange of personal trifles had been effected; watches and seals, cigar-cases, pencils, pocket-books, all had been changed, evidently because they bore upon them some clue to the owner's identity. In Tor's pocket-book, which had been left behind, was a sealed packet, which, to Phil's great astonishment, contained English bank-notes to the value of £500.

He looked utterly amazed, and then his face clouded.

'Is it a bribe? or is it a trap?—I cannot tell. But if I can escape, this money will be everything in my chance of success. Ah! and here is a paper—what can this be?'

It was the lawyer's letter informing Phil of his accession to wealth and property. The very reading of it, with the associations called up by the various items of intelligence, was enough to set Phil's heart beating with impatient longing. The other papers Tor had taken away with him, so that Maud's letter and Mr. Maynard's could explain nothing; although in them lay the clue to Tor's reckless deed.

Phil placed everything exactly as he had found it, and lay down again to meditate.

His plan—the plan which for days and days had been slowly shaping itself in his brain, was this: He must escape from his present captivity, but must escape in such a way that no uneasiness should be excited in Tor's mind— he must remain in ignorance of the matter.

Once free from restraint and with money in his pocket, Phil would go in disguise to Ladywell, and watch what the enemy was about. He could then calculate what were his chances of success, should he bring an action against him; and he might possibly be able to detect some extenuating circumstances which should make the crime less black.

Not willingly had Phil believed his friend a traitor; and there still lurked in his heart some hopes of a future reconciliation. But doubt and distrust were very strong, and the feeling of helplessness most trying. Tor had taken possession of every credential Phil could have brought forward as proof of his identity, and, as it were, cut away the ground from under his feet in every possible way.

Phil knew nothing of his likeness to his family, and was not man of the world enough to see that his own knowledge and recollection of the events of his childhood and of his native place, as opposed to Tor's ignorance, would go far towards making good his case, were it brought before competent authority. He could only see at present that it would be his bare word, against Tor's word backed by all the credentials which should have been his. He knew Tor would be no mean opponent, and his heart sank at the thought of a hand-to-hand fight.

No, he must go disguised, whilst Tor believed him still in Germany, and then he would try to read the riddle; and if he dared, he would confront his false friend face to face, and wrest the truth from him by threat, or by sheer force of justice.

But this plan of escape involved the co-operation of the German doctor, in whose care he had been left; and it might be a difficult, even a dangerous matter to secure it.

However, Phil was not without a certain dogged obstinacy of his own, and he determined that he would at least make a bold attempt, and trust to chance for success.

Upon the following day, when the doctor visited him, he received him with wide-open eyes, and a look of quiet comprehension, which sent the little man into a silent ecstasy of delight.

'Dr. Schneeberger,' began Phil, after he had calmly and rationally replied to some dozen searching questions, 'will you sit down for a few minutes and listen to something of importance that I have to say?'

'Certainly, my dear sir, certainly. I am only too delighted. What news this will be for your good friend! I think I ought to send him a telegram at once to inform him.'

'Not just yet, if you please, doctor,' said Phil quietly; 'I want you first to hear what I have to say to you.'

'I will listen to anything, so long as you do not too greatly fatigue yourself.'

'I will be careful not to do so. Now, doctor, I am going to ask you a few questions. Was I not brought here several weeks ago by a tall, good-looking Englishman, who gave his name as Debenham? And did he not inform you that my name was Torwood?'

Dr. Schneeberger nodded his head.

'Certainly—exactly. You have accurately stated the case.'

'And did he, or did he not, warn you that when I recovered my senses, I should be under the impression that *my* name was Debenham?'

The doctor stared.

'Well—ah! let me see—well, yes, he certainly did give me some such warning; but I cannot imagine how you came to know it.'

He was looking very curiously at his patient, as if to detect some new and strange phenomenon in his case. But Phil confronted him with an unwavering eye, and spoke on connectedly and quietly.

'I know it, or guessed it, from what I know of the circumstances which surround me, and from what I heard and remarked whilst I seemed to you to be still unconscious.'

'You have recovered, then, gradually?' cried the doctor eagerly. 'It was not the work of a moment?'

'I have been slowly recovering for several days; but this is the first time that I have felt any inclination to rouse myself and let it be known. You have doubtless known similar cases?'

Dr. Schneeberger assented readily, and talked a good deal of the brain and its various developments. Phil listened with praiseworthy patience, until a pause gave him the opportunity to proceed.

'When this friend of mine informed you that he considered it probable I should claim the name of Debenham upon my recovery, did it not strike you as a very odd thing for him to suppose?'

'Well, yes; certainly it was a remarkable symptom, one which interested me greatly.'

'Did you ever know of a case in which, after the brief confusion of ideas on first recovery, a man did not know his own name?'

'Well, no; I certainly have not known of such a case; but one is always making fresh discoveries in the book of Nature.'

'Or of art,' suggested Phil. 'And now, doctor, your candid opinion: do you think it likely, do you consider it practically possible, for a man to recover the full use of his faculties, and yet not to know who he is?'

The doctor hummed and hawed a little, but admitted that it seemed rather an improbable idea, when looked at in that light.

'I want you to look at it in this light; not simply from a medical point of view. Treat me as a man, not as a patient, and tell me if it never occurred to you what could be the reason for such a statement on the part of my friend.'

'He said it had occurred before, and might recur in this instance.'

'And it never struck you as possible that I might really be Philip Debenham, and he the Torwood he wished to make me out?'

The doctor stared, and eyed him suspiciously.

'No, certainly; such an idea as that never occurred to me for a moment.'

'Think over the idea for a moment, doctor, and see what you make of it.'

Dr. Schneeberger looked puzzled, and seemed to turn the matter over in his mind, looking all the while meditatively at Phil.

'You see that I know what I am saying?'

'Yes, you certainly do that.'

'I am talking to you now in a foreign tongue. I am ready to answer any and every question you like to put upon any subject with which I am acquainted. I can tell you, as I mean to do, the whole of my past history, or talk to you in half a dozen languages. Do you think it is possible that I do not know my own name?'

'It seems improbable; but we will have your friend over, and hear all he has to say. Why should he say he is a Debenham if he is not?'

'He had a very adequate motive, as I will show you. My name gained for him wealth and position, and landed property of considerable value. I will tell you all about it immediately; but first promise me one thing—not to write yet to my friend to tell him of the change in my state. You must promise me this.'

'But I promised him——'

'Never mind that promise now. Wait at least until you have heard my story. One day cannot make much difference. You will do dreadful mischief if you do not listen to me.'

The poor little man, unused to face difficulties of this kind, gave way without much demur.

'I will hear your story, at least. That cannot do harm, nor lose much time. If it will not tire you, mein Herr, I am ready to listen to it now.'

So Phil began the story of his life, and told it clearly and consecutively from beginning to end. He told of his eccentric great-uncle and the Ladywell property, to which he was natural heir. He told all the family history, and was too clear and succinct to speak from mere hearsay. Finally, he told of his awakening from this strange sleep, to find that the property had suddenly become his own, and that his trusted friend and comrade had played Jacob's part toward him, and had supplanted him in his inheritance.

CHAPTER IV.
ESCAPE.

BY the time Phil had finished his story, his listener was quite convinced that he was in his right mind, and that he spoke the truth.

He had tested him by questions likely to confuse a mind not perfectly clear, but Phil had answered everything with perfect readiness, and had avoided any of those blunders or contradictions which any hallucination must have occasioned.

Dr. Schneeberger, though simple-minded, was a shrewd observer of human nature, and he was convinced that Phil's story was true, and that he was the victim of gross injustice at the hands of his supposed friend.

Tor, he said to himself, just looked like a man who would dare anything, and make everything and everybody give way before him. He had been pleased before by his open, authoritative manner; but now it struck him as an index to a wild, unregulated nature.

Friendship was a sacred thing in the eyes of this little German, and he was much horrified at this cruel desecration just revealed to him.

'Dr. Schneeberger,' said Phil, 'you see, I think, that it is necessary for me to escape from the power of this false friend.'

'Are you in his power?'

'I fear I shall find myself so. He will compass everything rather than give me liberty to speak the truth before the world. Can you not see for yourself how he has manœuvred to keep me in his power? He told you I was given to delusions as to my identity. He urged you to send for him the moment I showed any glimmer of consciousness. Does it not all point to the one conclusion that his aim is to make me out an imbecile, and so retain control over my movements?'

'It may be so,' answered the doctor slowly; 'but yet he did not look like playing so base a part.'

'No; he had barely taken the first step then. Now he has plunged recklessly into the mire of treachery and deceit. Think for yourself, doctor—if he is capable of assuming my name and my inheritance, is he not capable also of doing much to keep me from exposing him?'

Dr. Schneeberger shook his head gravely.

'I cannot say it is impossible. I fear you have only too good cause for all you say.'

'You would indeed say so more emphatically still, did you but know Mr. Torwood's strength of will, and his power of bending circumstances and individuals to it. I stand in no small danger—of that I am convinced; and I must act at once, and that secretly. I have a plan, but I shall want your help in carrying it out. Will you stand my friend, doctor?'

'I will, mein Herr, as far as possible.'

'Your part is simple. All you have to do is to let me leave your roof, without letting the would-be Mr. Debenham know. He must suppose me to be here, whilst really I shall be watching him at close quarters.'

'Watching him! Will you then run into danger by going near to him?'

'I shall go disguised. I have money: I can soon so alter myself that none will know me. My beard has grown, and that in itself is a great disguise. I hardly knew myself when I saw my own reflection for the first time. I must watch the enemy at close quarters before I can strike. I must find out his weak points, and see if there are any in my old neighbourhood who will stand my friends. I must be on the spot; but it must be impossible for him to suspect who I am. You must write from time to time to say that I am here, and continue in the same unconscious state. He *cannot* then suspect.'

Dr. Schneeberger considered this proposition awhile, and then slowly shook his head.

'It will not do,' he said. 'It would be dangerous for us both. Any time the Herr might take it into his head to come over and visit you—I wonder he has not done so already. Suppose he came and found you away, what then would happen?'

Phil looked blank as this idea was propounded. The suggestion was reasonable enough, and showed him more and more how much of a prisoner he was.

'What, then, can be done?'

The doctor sat in deep thought. This time it was from him that the suggestion came.

'Mein Herr, does your friend know much of the science of medicine?'

'Not an atom, I should imagine.'

'Then it would not occur to him, perhaps, as an odd method of treating supposed compression of the brain, to send the patient upon a sea-voyage?'

Phil's eyes brightened slowly.

'No, doctor; I don't suppose it would. Go on.'

'Anyone who had studied the subject would not be likely to approve such an experiment; but if your friend does not understand these matters, I could easily lead him to suppose that such a course of treatment would be beneficial to you, and he might be willing for you to go.'

'And then?' questioned Phil eagerly.

'And then, mein Herr, whilst you were supposed to be sailing over the wide ocean, under the care of a medical friend of mine own, you could in reality be playing the part you have laid down for yourself; whilst I, for my part, could forward to the Herr letters, purporting to come from my friend, with accounts of Herr Torwood's health. As they would be written to me, no envelopes need be sent; and I could fabricate the date, and the port from which it was written, as easily as the letter itself with its medical details.'

'Doctor,' said Phil solemnly, 'you are a brick!—if you know what that is. Write to Ladywell this afternoon; don't lose a single day nor hour. Propound this idea of the sea-voyage, and urge it so that in common humanity he can hardly refuse.'

'I will,' answered the doctor, who could be a warm partizan when he once espoused a cause. 'And now, mein Herr, I think you had better return to your former state of torpor. It will not be well for Gretchen or the Mädchen to know that this change has taken place; only we ourselves must be in the secret. But I will write at once to Herr Debenham.'

Tor's answer came as quickly as post could bring it, and contained the information that he was following his letter with all speed.

For one moment Phil was filled with a great longing to meet his old friend face to face, and ask him, then and there, what was the meaning of this strange treachery; but soon the new fear and distrust rose up again within him—the knowledge of the power Tor always had exercised over him (to which in old days he had loved to submit, and which had always been generously exercised) came back to his memory, and made him fear to meet him; for there could be no doubt that the old generosity and friendliness must all have vanished, and given place to a malice and treachery which would make him a most dangerous enemy.

And yet Phil's heart misgave him sometimes, and smote him for the part he was about to play. True, he had been greatly wronged, ruthlessly betrayed and deceived; but did that justify him in deceiving, in his turn, the man to whom he owed so much?

Phil felt restless and miserable as he turned over the question in his mind.

'If he calls me "Phil" again, as he used to do, I don't believe I can hold out. Oh, Tor, Tor! why are you treating me like this?'

Sounds in the hall below announced the arrival of the expected guest. Phil, with a hasty movement, drew the sheet over the lower part of his face, so as to hide the beard, upon which he was to rely in a great measure for his disguise. Then he lay motionless and rigid, with closed eyes and set face.

He knew that Tor was standing over him, but he moved not an eyelash, although his heart beat so loud as to drown the sense of what was passing between the two men who stood beside the bed.

'He is going to speak to me,' said Phil to himself, when first he was able to grasp the meaning of words uttered in that familiar voice. 'What will he say?'

'Tor—Torwood! wake up, old fellow! Don't you know me—Phil Debenham? Tor, I say!'

Phil's heart seemed turned to stone, and he lay still and motionless. Hope died within him as suddenly as it had leapt up. Tor had adopted his *rôle* in earnest, and he would abide by his choice. By stratagem, not by force, was he now to be overcome.

On the following day Tor departed, and upon the next, Phil did the same. Greatly to his relief, no mention had been made of the money so strangely left in the pocket-book. Either Tor had forgotten the matter, or else he had his own reasons for keeping silence. Phil cared little as to that, so long as he retained in his hands the necessary funds for his enterprise.

He was carried from the doctor's house like a log, and his host accompanied him in the carriage. By the time he reached the wayside inn, where a halt was called, the doctor assisted him to alight and dismissed the driver, who merely observed that the sick man had recovered somewhat during the drive. He was not the man usually employed by Dr. Schneeberger, and knew nothing about him or his charge.

Once at the inn, Phil recovered rapidly, and by four o'clock the doctor and he bid each other a cordial adieu; and the former returned to his house, to give the innocent Gretchen a graphic account of the journey, and to tell her that his patient had been duly handed over to the mythical medical friend, who was to convey him down to the ship.

As for Phil, he felt like a bird escaped from the snare of the fowler, rejoicing once again in the full use of his liberty.

He remained that night where he was, for he had a vague fear that too rapid travelling might bring him into collision with Tor, and he was anxious above all things not to risk an encounter with him, until the right moment had arrived.

His disguise occupied much of his thought and attention, and he determined to go to Paris to obtain it; having unbounded faith in French art.

He made a wise choice; and Paris certainly turned him out a vastly altered man.

First, his brown beard was cut in truly foreign fashion, and dyed an inky black. A costly wig of raven-black hair, of distinct Italian style, so altered the character of brow and face, that Phil hardly knew his own reflection in the glass. Art had no difficulty in darkening his eyebrows and giving them an arch not actually intended by nature; and a pair of gold-rimmed glasses with smoked lenses gave a totally altered expression to the one feature he feared would betray him.

One or two carefully padded coats, of distinct Parisian cut, gave a breadth and solidity of figure quite unlike Phil's own slight and wiry proportions, and transformed him into a foreigner quite as much as did the Italian hair.

'Well, I'm not a bad-looking fellow, at any rate,' said he, carefully surveying his reflected image, when all his preparations were complete. 'But I'm hanged if I should know myself if I were to meet myself in the street. A few more applications of that fellow's wash will produce a clear olive complexion, and I don't think I need be afraid then of Tor or anybody else. I look most like an Italian, so an Italian I'll be. I think I'm equal to the language. I was always told I spoke it like a native, and I don't feel as if I could easily be puzzled. Yes, I'll be an Italian, and my name shall be—shall be—say Pagliadini, Marco Pagliadini; that will do as well as any other.'

Since his metamorphosis, he had left his first hotel, and just arrived at a second, in the empty *salon* of which he now stood, surveying himself in the long mirrors.

A confusion of tongues became audible in the hall without, and a waiter put his head into the *salon*, and then advanced with a bow.

'Is it possible that Monsieur is an Italian?' he asked obsequiously.

'Yes, certainly,' answered Phil, with a half-smile at his own readiness.

'Then might I solicit the aid of Monsieur for one of his compatriots, who cannot make himself to be comprehended in our language? If Monsieur would have the complaisance to go to his assistance, I am sure he would receive a thousand thanks.'

Phil assented readily, and found a fine-looking old Italian in the hall, vainly trying to make known his wishes to the mistress of the hotel; but his command of the French tongue was not great enough to make her understand that he had been taking photographs of some neighbouring landscapes, and was now anxious to expose his negatives in a dark cellar.

With Phil's assistance, however, the matter soon became amicably settled, and the Italian, in his gratitude to his young countryman, insisted on his company at dinner that night.

Phil spent a very pleasant evening with Signor Mattei, his intelligent and courteous host, who, after much talk of art, during which Phil rose higher and higher in his estimation, began to question him a little as to his own plans.

'I am going to England,' Phil told him candidly. 'I have not been there since I was quite a child. I am curious to see something of so great a country.'

'Are you going to visit friends?'

'No; I go simply as a traveller, bent on pleasure and instruction.'

'But you surely have introductions?'

'No, not even an introduction. I shall be a stranger to everyone I meet.'

'Surely that will be very *triste*?'

'If so, I can but return.'

Signor Mattei pulled his long white moustache and considered awhile.

'You have done me a very kind service, young Signor,' he said. 'I should like, if it were possible, to be of some service to you; but unfortunately I know little of England or the English.'

'I am exceedingly obliged by your kind wish, Signor; but pray do not give any anxiety to such a matter. I shall make my way excellently, I have no doubt. I am not afraid.'

Still Signor Mattei seemed to ponder.

'I suppose, Signor, you will not be going into remote parts—into the West-country, for instance, where the scenery is said to be very beautiful?'

'Well, yes; I am thinking of visiting Devonshire. I was there as a child, and should like to see the country again.'

'In that case I might perhaps be of use to you. A very good friend and relative of mine (by marriage, you understand, for he is an Englishman) lives in that country, at a place called Ladywell. His name is Michael Meredith, and when my niece, his wife, died, he returned to his native country, to live near an old patron of his, a Mr. Debenham, who also lived there. He is a great lover of art, and of all that belongs to our country. He is blind, which is a sad trial to him, and would make a visit from one of our nation doubly grateful. If you would accept an introduction to him, I am sure it would be doing a kindness to him, and might be advantageous to yourself.'

This marvellous coincidence had almost taken Phil's breath away. Michael Meredith's name was dimly remembered by him; and he accepted with alacrity the offered introduction.

What wonderful luck he had!

The one difficulty he had seen looming before him was now overcome.

He had wondered how he should be able to gain the first footing amongst the people he was so anxious to watch.

He could not hang about the place for ever, though sketching or fishing might give colour to a good deal of loitering round. But, as a rule, foreigners do not remain very long in isolated country villages, for no ostensible reason. Suspicion might be attracted to him, which he was most anxious to avoid; and it might be very difficult for him to gain the *entrée* of his own house.

Now, however, his way was made plain. He would appear at Ladywell as Michael Meredith's friend. Not a ghost of a suspicion could attach to him, unless he chose to arouse it. Tor, as a supposed Debenham, must be acquainted with his father's old friend, and a meeting would be easily contrived. Nothing more fortunate could have been conceived, and Phil felt as if victory was almost attained, when Signor Mattei handed over to him a very cordial note of introduction to Michael Meredith.

'I trust it may be of use to you, Signor,' he said politely.

'I have no doubt of it,' answered Phil, as calmly as he could. 'I shall make an early expedition to Devonshire to see the Signor Meredith.'

'You will do him a great kindness, I am convinced,' said Signor Mattei.

'And myself also,' responded Phil truthfully enough; and the elder man bowed and smiled, and was all the more favourably impressed by the courteously-worded thanks of his young friend.

The two 'compatriots' parted soon afterwards upon the best of terms.

When Phil read through the open letter which the Signor had given him, he was pleased to find it so worded, as to give the impression that Signor Pagliadini was no mere acquaintance of an hour, but a friend of some standing. Signor Mattei, with a somewhat exaggerated wish to speak well of his young friend, had thought it best not to give any hint as to the length of time the friendship had lasted, and leave the date of its commencement to the imagination of his relative. From what he said of Phil's knowledge of art, and his taste upon all questions relating to painting and sculpture, one would certainly imagine that the two men had been acquainted for some time. He had also omitted to date the letter from Paris, and so it might naturally be supposed to come from Florence, where, as Phil had discovered, the Signor habitually resided.

'It's not a matter of much importance, I suppose,' he said to himself: 'still, it's as well to throw as much dust in people's eyes as one easily can. It might just as well be supposed that I have come direct from Florence, so that if Tor should ask questions he will not learn the truth.'

He paced up and down, speaking from time to time to himself.

'I won't be harder upon him than I can—I don't want to disgrace him. He has been a good friend to me; and I will be as generous as he will let me. But I cannot stand by altogether and see myself supplanted. I cannot change myself into Torrington Torwood because he has chosen to make himself Phil Debenham.

'I will feel my way carefully. I will say that I have known the two abroad. Perhaps I will even greet him as Torwood, and see what he says. That might be a good thought, and might give him an opening to confess the truth. I might put the same doubt into other people's minds, and let an uncomfortable state of uncertainty fall upon them in regard to his position. I am sure I shall not be recognised. I will speak no English, only Italian, and then my voice will be in a great measure disguised. I will haunt him and trouble him, and give him every chance to retract his false step and tell the truth; but if he will not yield, even when he finds that I know the truth, then I must take up arms in my own defence; and he must look to himself.

'Oh, Tor! Tor!' cried Phil, with sudden, irrepressible bitterness. 'Why do you drive me into such a course? Why do you make an enemy of me—I who have so loved you? Oh, Tor! Tor! Mine own familiar friend!'

CHAPTER V.
FIRST EXPERIENCES.

IT was with very strange and mixed feelings that Philip Debenham found himself once again in his native village.

The place was almost unchanged by the eighteen years that had passed since he had seen it last. A few cottages had vanished; a few more had been built. His old home had been altered past recognition; but little else was changed, so far as the larger houses were concerned.

He saw the well-known, square, uncompromising mansion of his Uncle Belassis, and gave it a look of instinctive aversion, remembering dimly the unhappy hours he had spent there as a boy.

He recognised with a smile the grey, ivycovered church which he had attended as a child, and could even recall the subjects of the stained windows which he had so admired, and recollect the half-fearful, half-delighted interest he and Maud used to take in a carved death's head and cross-bones, which surmounted one of the tablets facing the pew in which they had sat.

A great longing rose up within him to see again the little sister, who had been his playfellow and devoted slave in the far-away childhood's years. Where was she now? Living still at Thornton House? Tor could not have brought her to Ladywell, he thought—odd as it might seem not to do so. He would have given much for one loving kiss from Maud, for one of the caresses he knew were his due; but he was a stranger and an alien, and could only come in disguise to see his own inheritance.

Ladywell lay embosomed in woods, which now wore their full summer foliage. He could not see his own house, and yet the very thought that it was his own, thrilled him with a pride and delight he had not felt before.

He remembered well the fine old place he had visited from time to time with his father. He could see, with his mind's eye, the great terrace, the smooth lawns, and brilliant flowerbeds; the hot-houses and conservatories, and the fine stables where he had loved to wander, petting and admiring the horses who were stalled there.

The inside of the house he remembered less vividly, but the idea of size and magnificence was strongly stamped upon his brain; and he heaved a sigh at the thought which rose in his mind, that his accession to his own property could only be obtained by the disgrace of the man who had once been his dearest, almost his only friend.

'What's that fine place?' asked a fellow-traveller, of the driver, as the conveyance which had brought them both from Darwen drove up to the village.

'Ladywell Manor, sir—finest place in the county.' For the village people were loyal in their admiration of their own Manor House.

'Who owns it?'

'Old Squire were Mr. Maynard—a queer old gentleman by all accounts, who never saw nobody. He never was married, and left the place to his nephew, Mr. Debenham. He's main popular is the new Squire, though he's not long come back from his travels; a pleasant-spoke, free-handed young gentleman as ever trod shoe-leather, and as strong and big as John the blacksmith, and he's the biggest man down these parts.'

'Is he a married man?—the Squire, I mean, not the blacksmith.'

'No, he ain't married not yet. He's been a-knocking about the world, they say, till now, and hasn't hardly had time to turn round, so far. He's got his aunt living up there now, a widow lady, and his sister; but he won't want for a wife long. Why, he's the best match in the country-side, to say nothing of his good looks. Oh yes, sir, we're a bit proud of our new Squire. You see, the old un wasn't greatly thought on; and this here Mr. Debenham, he's the right sort all round. There's not a soul in all Ladywell as hasn't a good word for the Squire, or who wouldn't stand up for him through thick and thin, so as he needed it.'

This conversation, casually overheard, had given Phil a good deal of food for meditation.

'It is plain he has not let grass grow under his feet,' he thought. 'He has played the old trick—won the hearts of the people to strengthen his own position. Who could have thought it of Tor? Yet what else can I think? Facts speak for themselves.'

That evening and the following morning he spent in restless wanderings and anxious thought.

He could not talk to the people, because he wished to make out that his English was of the most imperfect kind; and, with all his brooding and thinking, he could not decide upon a regular plan of action.

The Debenham indecision was in his nature, and there was now no Tor at his side to give ready advice and assistance. He had for the first time to stand alone and act for himself, and all he could make up his mind to do, was to drift along with the tide of circumstances, and be guided by his own impulse what to say and what to leave unsaid.

It was not perhaps a very wise resolve, but it was eminently characteristic of Phil's habit of mind. Had Mr. Belassis had his real nephew to deal with from the first, things might have turned out very differently for all parties concerned.

In this indecisive frame of mind Phil stood at Mr. Meredith's door, and was admitted to Roma's studio.

Roma, as Tor had said to Maud, possessed that type of beauty which Phil most admired, and the longer they talked the greater grew his admiration.

The bust of Maud in the studio at once arrested his attention, and he saw at a glance whose portrait it must be, from its obvious likeness to himself. Given this opening, he followed it up, talking of the Filippo he had once known, making up his mind that he would contrive to make Tor pretty uncomfortable.

His next interview, with Mr. Meredith, was very satisfactory. From the first moment it was evident he had made a favourable impression. Something in his voice fell pleasantly and familiarly upon the sensitive ear of the blind man, and caused him to assert more than once that he must have met Signor Pagliadini before.

When the introduction from Signor Mattei was brought forward, Phil had himself to read it to the blind man. By a dexterous and very slight transposition and alteration, the impression conveyed by the letter was, that Marco Pagliadini was quite an old friend, and had been known to Signor Mattei from his youth upwards.

The invitation to become an inmate at Michael Meredith's was very welcome, and was so warmly pressed that it had not to be too eagerly accepted. Fortune certainly seemed to favour Phil, for as a guest in this house he could not fail to have many opportunities for making inquiries and finding out all that was possible about Tor's line of action. His former acquaintance with the two Englishmen, which he lost no time in making known, gave colour to the interest he could not but show in all connected with Ladywell, and especially in the actions of its present master.

He was ill pleased to find what warm allies he had made even in this house. Mr. Meredith was never tired of singing his praises, and even Roma threw off something of her usual calm to defend, when Phil made a covert attack upon him, the man who, did she but know it, so ill deserved her goodwill.

Tor's hasty disappearance, to avoid a meeting with anyone who had known him abroad, was a significant fact, and showed that he was really ill at ease, in spite of his popularity.

But that evening spent in company with Roma lulled into temporary oblivion all thoughts of anger or vengeance. Roma was, in his opinion, the most beautiful woman he had ever met, and his somewhat fervent nature was soon all ablaze with the ardour of a dangerous admiration, all the more dangerous because Roma seemed with every hour to grow more gentle, more pensive, more trustful.

He almost forgot the object of his visit in the happiness of her society, and he was far upon the way from which there is no retreat, before the first evening had passed. It seemed to him that his one object in coming to England had been to find Roma, and that to win her love was now the only object worth living for.

But his thoughts were turned into a different channel the next day, by a visit Maud paid to her friend's studio.

Phil was with Roma, watching her work, for Michael Meredith was not yet down; and the young man forgot, as did also Roma, the foreign ideas of fitness of things, and assumed an English freedom, which seemed to them quite natural and proper under the circumstances.

'I am expecting Miss Debenham for a sitting. She promised to come this morning. You will see then if she so resembles her brother.'

Phil, so to speak, pricked up his ears.

'Miss Debenham coming here?'

'Yes, Signor.'

'May I be permitted to stay? Will she or you think it too great an intrusion? I should so like some converse with my old friend's sister.'

'Maud will be delighted, I am sure. She is the merriest girl in the world, and adores her brother. Any friend of his will be welcome.'

There was the sound of a light footfall down the long passage.

'Here she is!' said Roma.

Maud entered, a fair vision, in her white dress and shady hat, with her bright eyes, clear, rose-tinted skin, happy smile and ready laugh.

'Roma! Here I am, you see! Not so late as usual. Oh, I beg your pardon. Are you engaged?'

'No; this is our friend Signor Pagliadini, who is visiting us, and is anxious to be presented to you. He knew your brother in Italy.'

On hearing this, Maud's face lighted up brightly, and she held out her hand.

'I am always pleased to see any friend of my brother's.'

There was an unconscious, fond pride in the way she spoke the words 'my brother,' which brought a keen sense of pain to Phil's heart.

It was hard, he felt, looking into his sister's face, after eighteen long years of separation, that it was but a stranger's welcome he received, and that its cordiality was only due to the fact that she believed him to be Tor's friend.

He was glad that he had not to say much, glad that she was unable to converse freely with him, and glad that preparations for the sitting were at once commenced.

Poor Phil was not endowed with any very large amount of self-control, and to meet thus his only sister, and a sister whom he had greatly loved, was a hard task, and one which roused in his heart all the bitterness which had been nearly lulled to sleep.

Time, however, brought him calmness, and he was soon able to listen to what the two girls were saying, whilst he appeared to be looking over some books of photographs. Roma knew that he could understand, although he could not speak English, so he was not afraid of taking an unfair advantage of his position.

'Isn't Phil a dear boy?' Maud was saying, with her usual enthusiasm. 'He says if things go on smoothly, he'll take Aunt Olive and me to Italy in the winter. Won't that be lovely! I do so want to travel, and I've never been out of England. He would have taken us to Switzerland this summer, only it's too soon, he thinks, for him to go away; and there's my birthday to get over, you know. But another summer he'll take us, and he'll let me do some mountaineering, he says. Won't that be splendid! I should love to go up Mont Blanc, or the Matterhorn, or some really big mountain. I believe Phil's done all the hardest. He's just the most wonderful boy in the world.'

Roma let her talk on in her favourite strain, glad to catch the animated expression such conversation always gave to her. She wound up by her favourite and well-worn phrase:

'Isn't he just an angel-boy, Roma?'

'He is very kind and good.'

Maud laughed, and shook her head

'Ah, you don't understand a bit. Lots and lots of people might be kind and good, but nobody could be like my Phil. I'm sure there isn't such another brother in all the world. I can't think now, however I managed to live without him.'

Roma smiled at her enthusiasm. Signor Pagliadini's face was turned away.

'It's quite true, and you needn't laugh. And oh, Roma, do you know what he is going to give me for a birthday present?'

'No. What?'

'A horse; a horse for my very own. Such a little beauty! You know those at Ladywell are all his, and are very nice; but he never gave one to me, though I ride them just as I like. I never thought of wanting one; but the other day the loveliest, sweetest, most delicious little horse appeared in one of the empty loose boxes. I happened to see him, and asked Phil. First he wouldn't tell me, and said I'd no business to play the spy; but I coaxed and coaxed, and at last he gave in. He said it was there on approval, and if its paces and temper and everything else were right, he was going to give him to me on my birthday. He said he had been looking out for a horse for me for a long time. He thought I must wonder why I had not had one before. As if I ever should!'

'What did you say?'

'Oh, I told him he was just a darling, and asked him why he didn't give me the horse I generally ride, who is quite nice in every way.'

'What did he say?'

'Oh, he laughed, and looked amused, and said he didn't mean to give away the Ladywell horses, not even to me. I didn't quite see why, I said; and he told me I should know better some day. Anyway, he's got me the loveliest little horse you can imagine—bay, with black points—and I love him ever so much already.'

Shortly after this Signor Pagliadini drew closer, and sat down near to sculptor and model, whilst he entered into conversation.

Maud was ready enough to talk, and, though a good deal of interpretation had to go on for form's sake, Phil felt that he was growing to know his sister better than she imagined.

He was ready enough, and she eager enough, to talk of the 'friend Filippo,' and poured out so many stories of his prowess and generosity, that poor Phil was quite dismayed to find how he had been supplanted in Maud's affection, and felt that she would not readily transfer her love to him.

Maud liked the dark foreigner with his somewhat sad, appealing eyes. Some subtle sympathy seemed to draw them together; and, impossible as she knew it to be, she could not help fancying she had known him before, at some far-distant period.

Some of the tones of his voice and the turns of expression made her fancy this; but rack her brains as she would, she could find nothing to account for the odd idea. It was out of the question that they ever could have met before.

A servant came to say that Mr. Meredith was down, and would be obliged if Signor Pagliadini would join him in his study.

Maud gave him her hand again, as he rose to obey the summons.

'If you knew my brother once, I wish you would come up to Ladywell this afternoon, and have tea with us. He will be delighted, I am sure, to renew the acquaintance.'

'I shall be most happy to do so, if the Signorina is sure I shall not intrude.'

'Quite sure,' answered Maud brightly. '*Au revoir*, then. Remember, you will be expected.'

'Who is he, Roma?' she asked, when he had gone.

'A friend of an uncle of my mother's, in Florence. He sent him here.'

'He is nice, is he not?'

'I think so.'

'And very good-looking?'

'Yes.'

'I can't think who he reminds me of. It quite bothered me whilst he was talking; not a likeness, you know, but just a look every now and then. Why, yes, I know now!'

'What?'

'There's a look in his eye like the picture of papa, in Aunt Olive's room. That's what it is. I'm glad I've remembered. I can't bear being puzzled like that—it's so irritating.'

And so Philip Debenham was to go in disguise to his own house, and meet, face to face, the man who was personating him.

It was a trying situation certainly, and some little cleverness and resolution was required in the carrying out of his part.

Phil did not lack cleverness, but his uncertainty and irresolution boded ill for his wish to carry things off with a high hand.

He believed Tor, warned of his visit, would contrive to meet him alone, and of this he was glad; and he had little fear that his disguise would be penetrated. It was peculiarly good, and lacked any sign of the grotesque which so often, in such cases, defeats its own object, by provoking suspicion and curiosity.

He looked so completely the Italian of rank and wealth, that he almost at times believed himself to be what he represented; and Tor, who *knew* that his friend was upon the open sea, could have no reason for suspicion.

Phil, as has been recorded, began boldly; but it was by a strong effort that he did so. When he stood face to face with his old friend his courage almost failed, and he was only withheld by distrust and fear from tearing off his disguise and calling out:

'Tor, old fellow! Here I am! What are you doing? and what am I to do?'

But he restrained himself, and spoke the more coldly and threateningly from his very agitation. He grew angry and desperate as he saw how coolly and calmly Tor stood his ground, and parried attacks which he thought would have forced him to lay down his arms.

To see this man standing before him, assuming his name and station, and almost scoffing at his well-aimed blows, was too much, and Phil felt lashed into fury.

He charged him straight out with wronging his friend; and then Tor gave such a bold, fearless denial to the charge, that, in spite of himself, Phil's distrust was shaken. It seemed his fate at this time to make up his mind that Tor was a villain, only to have this conviction shaken by some earnest assurance or chance discovery; and then, hardly had the balance weighed down upon the side of friendship, before some new revelation would wake up all the old animosity and fear.

Tor's next asseveration, that he could hold his own against the world, and would defy all the innuendoes cast at him by anyone, was certainly a 'facer' after what had gone before; and Phil left Ladywell in as troubled and doubtful a state as he had entered it, and more and more convinced that Tor, with his strong will and high hand, would be no mean opponent, all the more dangerous for the general enthusiasm he seemed to inspire in others.

It behoved Phil to walk with great care, and to avoid raising suspicions in the minds of his hosts. Michael Meredith, however, was too much absorbed in his own dreams to give overmuch heed to what might be going on in other people's minds; and from him Phil could learn a great deal that was valuable to him, without running any risk.

He heard with a sort of satisfaction, that Tor had enemies in his supposed uncle and aunt, Mr. and Mrs. Belassis. Now Phil knew nothing absolutely conclusive against these relatives of his, save that he had not liked them as a child. His father, however, had been an intimate friend of Belassis, and his mother had been closely related to them.

Old Maynard's letter and Maud's, which would have given him the clue to the real character of his uncle, had never reached him, and he had not the faintest idea that any suspicion of dishonesty could attach to his name. All he knew was that he had feared and disliked his uncle as a boy, and had been very indignant when he had doomed him to an office-stool instead of bringing him up 'as a gentleman.'

Time, however, had somewhat modified this feeling. Phil knew enough of the world now, to be aware that a penniless youth of family has a better chance of rising in the world by beginning life at a merchant's desk, than in any capacity that he would have selected for himself; and he could forgive the uncle for the choice he had made. At the same time, he could not shake off the impression that he had been unfairly treated by being so long banished from home, and not allowed to see his sister or any other relative; and he knew that Maud had been anything but content with her life under her uncle's roof.

All these considerations rose up one by one before him, and he could not yet say whether or not he would take advantage of their dislike to Tor to make allies of the Belassis'. Instinct warned him not to trust them. Reason told him that his wisest plan would be to get his nearest relatives upon his side.

CHAPTER VI.
THE WISHING WELL.

PHIL'S perplexities, however, did not trouble him much, when once he found himself in the quiet seclusion of Meredith's house.

Implicitly trusted by the blind man, and liked by his daughter, Phil found himself wonderfully at home there, and with every hour a deeper contentment settled upon his spirit.

He wandered with Roma that evening in the dewy, moonlit garden, and neither remembered to wonder what it was that made the quiet hour so sweet. To neither did the sudden intimacy which had grown up between them seem strange. Rather it appeared as if they had known one another all their lives.

'Or in another life before this one, Roma,' said Phil, as they stood looking at the stars together. He had accidentally called her 'Roma' before now, and neither had observed what seemed so natural. 'Surely this life is not the first. Do you not often feel that long, long ago you have lived out a previous existence—somewhere?'

'I suppose everyone has some such feeling from time to time,' answered Roma dreamily. 'Only we cannot be sure of it.'

'Why do we want to be sure? Why should we not be content to dream and to wonder? Certainty does not bring satisfaction—rather the reverse. Life is eternal, is it not—without beginning and without end? We must have lived before this. When we did so, I am sure that you and I were very near together. Does it not seem so to you, Roma?'

She smiled a little.

'Perhaps it does.'

'You feel it too; then there is no room for doubt. One life has been spent side by side—shall this one be so spent, too?'

The last words were little more than a whisper. He was not sure that she had heard, for her head was turned slightly aside.

'Have you no answer?' he asked, taking her hand, and forcing her to look at him.

'An answer?'

'Yes, Roma. You admit that we are not strangers really. Love knows no dates—time has no power over it. Days are as years, and years as days. We have known each other for years. You have said it yourself.'

'Not quite,' she answered gently. 'We were talking then of dreams and sweet fancies. Life, Signor, is not made up of these.'

'Signor!' he repeated reproachfully. 'How can you be so cold? Call me Filippo.'

'Filippo!' she repeated wonderingly.

'I mean Marco,' he answered, with a confusion which was not noticed in the darkness. 'I was thinking of my friend whom I saw this afternoon. Will you not call me Marco sometimes?'

'I—I do not know,' faltered Roma. 'I think—I think we ought not to stay here.'

'Why not? Is it unpleasant to you to be with me?'

'It is not that,' said Roma softly.

'Then we will stay,' answered Philip, taking her hand and placing it upon his arm. 'Come, let us go together to the park—Ladywell park—and look at the moonlight through the great trees. Your father is tired to-night, and will be best alone. Come, you shall tell me how you like Ladywell, and if——'

He pulled up there, but Roma answered softly:

'Ladywell is lovely—the loveliest place in the world, I think.'

He smiled, and said half to himself:

'You would be happy, then, to call it home?'

Roma took her hand away, and said in a pained voice:

'Do not talk so, Signor.'

He understood, he thought, what she would imply, and smiled to himself, well pleased.

They were now in the park, wandering amid the chequered lights and shades of the wooded hollows. Phil looked round him with a sense of recollection.

'Is there not a well somewhere here, Roma?—a wishing-well?'

'Yes; but how do you know?'

'I must have been here, I think, in that former life, of which we were talking just now. Full moon and a summer's night—is not this just the right time? Shall we go and wish there together now, Roma? Surely such an opportunity is not to be lost!'

She smiled an assent.

'Are you superstitious, Marco?'

He looked at her with a glad, proud smile.

'I think I could be so to-night.'

Phil led the way through the woodland path, down to the secluded well. He remembered the path as well as if he had only traversed it yesterday, and Roma forgot to be surprised.

It was in reality a spring, this so-called 'wishing-well:' a clear bubbling spring, rising up in a natural stone basin, lined with moss and fringed with fern. A quaint stone cup hung by a rusty iron chain beside the spring, and round the edge of the basin a quaint inscription was carved, stating the magic properties of the well.

Phil stood looking thoughtfully into the dimpling water, where faint reflected lights and shadows played, and then he took the cup and filled it.

'Have you a wish ready, Roma?'

'Yes.'

'Then wish and drink; for something within tells me that the hour is favourable, and the spirits propitious to our wishes.'

Roma smiled and drank, and Phil tossed the remaining drops upon the grass in a silvery shower, pronouncing a few mystic words.

'Why so?' asked Roma.

'We always used to do it——' there was a momentary pause—'in my country, at a fairy well, which my sister and I sometimes visited as children. But I must wish now, and the cup must not be used twice upon the same night. I must take the bolder course, and brave the wrath of the spirits. Do they not say that those who do so, gain a more generous fulfilment, or a marked repudiation of their wish?'

'How do you know?' asked Roma again.

'I suppose wishing-wells are pretty much the same all the world over,' he answered lightly. 'Anyway, I will be bold. Now for it!'

He bent his head over the sparkling spring, and took a long, deep draught. Then he stood upright, and his face looked earnest and steadfast.

'You have wished a long wish,' remarked Roma, when at length he moved.

'I have—a long and complex wish—so complex that I fear even the spirits of the well will find it hard to answer every part, even if they try.'

'You should have faith,' said Roma, smiling. 'To doubt them is fatal.'

'Then I will not doubt,' he answered quickly. 'I will believe they can accomplish all; but they have a hard task before them!'

Roma looked curiously at him.

'I wonder what you can have wished.'

'Something concerning my own personal history—you know we must not reveal our wishes.'

'Of course not,' she answered seriously; but as they lingered round the quiet spot, where the silence was only broken by the murmuring of the magic spring, Phil began again to speak, and Roma fancied he was still thinking of his complex wish.

'Now I want you to give me an opinion,' he said, 'for I am very much perplexed. Which should be the stronger claim upon us, the claim of justice or that of gratitude?'

'What do you mean?' asked Roma. 'It is a hard question, as you put it.'

'It is a hard question, put it as you will. I mean just what I say. When justice urges you to one course, and gratitude to another, which motive should be allowed to triumph?'

Roma's brow became knit by a frown of perplexity.

'It is not easy to decide without knowing more; but I think gratitude should be held very sacred.'

'And injustice allowed to go on?'

'Oh no; not quite that. Injustice can never, never be right. It should always be checked, if possible. Only gratitude should not be set on one side.'

'You answer by a paradox in this case. Either gratitude or justice must be set aside.'

'I cannot think but that both might be considered: there must be some right way of doing right—there always is. Can you not tell me more?'

'I can only tell you that one who was my friend, and to whom I owe much gratitude, has now turned traitor, and done me a grievous wrong. I must right myself before the world. I cannot submit to be defrauded of my all, to be made an outcast and a wanderer upon the face of the earth; but I can only do so by bringing disgrace upon the man I once loved well, and to whom I certainly owe a debt of gratitude.'

Roma pondered deeply. It seemed a hard case, and she scarcely knew what to advise.

'Is there no middle course?'

'I fear he will not accept a compromise. What I know of his character, and what I have heard of his actions, lead me to suppose that he will fight to the death, and leave me no option but to expose and disgrace him.'

'I suppose you have come to England for legal advice,' said Roma.

'Yes, and to take a calm and dispassionate view of things. It is an unpleasant position to be placed in, is it not?'

'Very indeed.'

'And have you no advice for me?'

'I'm afraid I know so little of the world that mine would be sadly unpractical.'

'Perhaps unworldly counsel might be better than that of the law,' answered Phil thoughtfully. 'Let me hear what you have to suggest, Roma.'

'Have you so quarrelled with this friend that you could not get speech of him?'

'Well—no, hardly that yet, I think; for I have only just learnt the injury he has done me.'

'Then I think I should go back and make him see me, and I should tell him that I did not want to harm him, but that justice must be done. I should say how it hurt me to have to fight anyone who had been good to me. I should say how grateful I still felt for his kindness; but I should be firm, and say at the same time, that if he *would* fight for the wrong instead of yielding to the right, I should be obliged to become his enemy.'

'It might be a dangerous step for me to take,' said Phil. 'For he is very strong.'

'What course are you thinking of pursuing?'

'I cannot make up my mind. A sudden blow would be most effective.'

'If he has ever been a friend to you, and if you owe him gratitude,' said Roma gravely, 'you ought not to strike him unawares. You owe it to him to be frank, even though he may have been treacherous to you. Never do wrong because another does it. You do not mind my speaking out?'

'No, indeed. I thank you for it, Roma; and I will take your advice. I had almost pledged myself to it before; now my mind is made up. Whatever is done shall be done openly, and my friend shall have due warning before I strike a blow.'

'I am sure you will never regret your decision,' said Roma warmly.

That episode of the wishing-well made a deep impression upon Phil and his companion. The mutual confidences they had exchanged seemed to draw them more closely together, and the secret which was known only to them, and which was to be inviolably kept, was a link which strengthened the bond between them.

'She is a noble woman and a sweet woman,' Phil said to himself that night. 'I will win her for my wife when I have my own again; and I think she will not shrink then at the idea of calling Ladywell her home. I can be paving the way with the father, though my lips are sealed at present, for I cannot give a false name and antecedents when I plead such a cause as that. With Roma, I cannot think my task will be a hard one. I am sure she is not indifferent to me. I think, too, she must know how I love her.'

It was not difficult to lead Michael Meredith to speak of his daughter. He was proud of her, and proud of any admiration bestowed upon her. He knew by the way in which his guest spoke and acted, that he had from the first been struck and impressed by Roma, and he was pleased that it was so.

'She has been my stay and solace all through my declining years,' said Meredith, in his studied, artificial way.

'I wonder you have kept her with you so long,' hazarded Phil.

'Ah, yes, you may say that with reason; but we have lived for one another, and apart from the world. Few men have even seen my Roma.'

'Rather hard on the men,' said Phil gallantly.

Meredith smiled, well pleased.

'Ah!' he said, 'but I knew my own mind. My choice was made before.'

'What do you mean, Signor?'

'I meant to choose her husband. Englishman though I am, I am foreigner enough to believe in marriages made by the parents. But I love my child, and would not willingly compel her fancy.'

Phil sat silent, and looked much taken aback. Meredith gently wandered on, as was his way when once started on a favourite theme.

'But I find, Signor, that a steady will and a gentle tact mould circumstances as well as individuals. I cannot act as other men do. I might even be held as helpless and dependent, and yet I find I have but to sit here and plan and *will*, and the rest follows of itself. I could say much upon that wonderful power—the human will.'

The monstrous egotism of the man passed unheeded; but his vague hints made Phil very uneasy.

'I do not know if I have followed you, Signor; do you mean that your will has brought to you such a husband as you have desired for your daughter?'

'Circumstances have brought the man; my will, or my child's charms have done the rest. I knew all would follow when he had appeared.'

Phil almost feared to ask the next question.

'Is the Signorina, then, already betrothed?'

'Yes, certainly.'

There was a brief pause before the next question.

'And may I ask to whom?'

'Oh yes; to our good friend Philip Debenham, the master of Ladywell Manor.'

'Ah!'

'You are surprised, it seems. Is it anything so very strange that he should love my child?'

'Why, no—oh no—not at all; but I did not know—I had not heard.'

'No, probably not. I have not alluded to the matter before, and young maidens do not speak of what lies so near to their hearts.'

'The Signorina is, without doubt, deeply attached to—to Signor Debenham.'

'Most deeply. It is a warm attachment on both sides. I perceived it from the first, long before the young people were aware of it themselves;' and Mr. Meredith smiled his quiet, satisfied smile.

'They have known each other long, no doubt?'

'Not very long; but time has little to do with such matters, as you may find out for yourself one day, Signor. It is we elders who think of time, and count the weeks the acquaintance has lasted, before giving our consent. But in this case I had no scruple. I had loved the father—I loved and trusted the son, and could give my daughter to him with my blessing.'

'For the sake of the father?' said Phil, in a strange, forced tone.

'First for the father's sake, then for his own. No one who owns the name of Debenham can but be dear to me.'

Phil mastered himself by an effort; but his silence had not passed unnoticed.

'I weary you by these personal details, Signor,' said Meredith courteously. 'I forget, in my blindness, that my little world is not all-absorbing to others. I hear Roma's voice in the garden. She will prove a pleasanter companion than I; and I will rest awhile, as I feel fatigued by this heat.'

With bitter feelings surging in his heart, Phil left the presence of the blind man.

'Is he not rightly called Jacob?' muttered he, in his wrath, recalling half-forgotten words which seemed now to burn themselves into his very brain. 'First he takes away my birthright, and now he takes away my blessing also.'

Roma was in the garden, singing softly to herself. She sang because she was happy, though why she was so, she did not pause to ask herself.

'Marco!'

The word seemed to escape her unawares, and her face brightened into a beautiful smile as she saw him.

'Roma!'

He had seen the look upon her face, and now he strode forward and seized her hands.

'Roma,' he said abruptly, 'I love you, and you know it. Do you love me?'

He was in earnest now, so much in earnest that all weakness and hesitancy had fled in a moment. He was stronger than she at the present moment, and his earnestness compelled her to answer, and to answer truly.

For a moment the nominal pledge that bound her was forgotten. Roma knew that she was really free, and that she had given her heart to this stranger.

'Yes, Marco,' she answered, lifting her dark eyes fearlessly to his, 'I love you.'

'My darling—my Roma!'

He drew her towards him, and she did not repulse him. Everything was for a brief space buried in oblivion, save the one all-important revelation that they loved one another.

Phil was the first to recover himself. After one pause of forgetfulness memory returned.

'Roma,' he said, 'I cannot believe my own happiness. I have won you in a moment of profound despair, just when I had heard from your father's lips that you were the promised bride of another. How has he made so great an error?'

The light died suddenly out of Roma's face, and her arms fell to her sides.

'I had forgotten,' she said hurriedly.

'Forgotten what?'

'That I am not free—yet.'

'Not free! Roma! Roma! And you have said that you love me!'

'I do love you, Marco. I cannot take back words I have spoken; but I had no right to speak them.'

'No right!'

'No; you know why—my father has told you.'

'You are betrothed to—Philip Debenham?'

She bent her head in a voiceless assent.

'Roma!' he cried, with pain and indignation in his tone, 'have you pledged your hand without your heart? or do you love this man?'

'You know I do not,' she answered proudly; 'I have told you whom I love.'

His face softened instantly.

'Forgive me, Roma. I should not have spoken so; but indeed you gave me cause. Let us come to your father now, and tell him all. Tell him you pledged yourself before you knew your own heart. We will kneel to him to grant what we ask, and to bless our love.'

But Roma shrank back with a frightened look.

'Oh no, no! Indeed you must not. It would kill him!'

'Kill him! He cannot care so very much.'

'He does! he does! Oh, Marco! you must have patience. If you cannot wait till I bid you speak, we must part now and for ever. I can die myself, but I cannot, I cannot give him such pain!'

Phil gazed at her in amazement.

'Roma, I cannot understand. Why should we wait? He must be told sometime—unless, indeed, you mean to sell yourself, and marry——'

'Oh no, no, Marco! how can you be so cruel? I will never marry him; but I cannot tell my father yet. You must trust me; you must be patient.'

'If only you would explain! How can things get anything but worse by waiting? I know Philip Debenham well, Roma. He will hold you to your promise through everything. He never gives way when once his mind is made up. You stand in great danger.'

Something in the warning tone made Roma tremble. Had the man she had believed in played her false? Would he hold her to her plighted word?

'Let me go in, Marco,' she said in low, trembling tones. 'I am very miserable. I don't know what to say or what to think. I do love you; but you must bear with me. Some day I will tell you all; till then you *must* keep silence. Think as kindly of me as you can. I must speak to Philip before I can speak to you any more of—of—love.'

She turned and left him, and Phil, with a dark look on his face, turned and shook his fist in the direction of Ladywell Manor.

'Torrington Torwood,' he said slowly and deliberately, 'I will make you pay for this!'

CHAPTER VII.
THE LAST STRAW.

IT was very well for Roma to tell Phil that he was not to speak again to her of love; but he was not at all prepared to submit to such a prohibition.

Roma loved him, and had admitted her love, therefore he had a right to assume towards her something of a lover's part.

'All is fair in love and war,' he said to himself; and he felt that against his false friend any step he chose to take was fair.

The fact that he had, by flattering the father's foolish vanity, obtained the promise of the daughter's hand against her own will, added fuel to the fire of his anger against Tor, which he had been able only fitfully to keep burning so far; and he now felt that he could proceed to severe measures with less scruple than heretofore.

Roma was unhappy; he saw that plainly through the evening hours that followed their declaration of mutual love; and the thought that Tor was making her suffer was enough to rouse, and to keep stirring within him, deep feelings of animosity and scorn.

Roma need not have been unhappy; but when a false position has been forced upon a woman, it must sooner or later become a trouble and an anxiety.

The girl had, in a great measure, forced herself into the position she thus occupied, by her feverish dread of agitating her father, by the promise she had obtained from Tor, and by her determination to sacrifice anything—her life's happiness, if need be—to his whims, which in her eyes were sacred.

It had seemed to her a trifling thing, this sacrifice, so long as no love had ever entered her life, save her love towards her blind father. She would even have made a loveless marriage rather than have given him pain, for she wrongly believed that her one duty in life was to shield him, at all cost, from any kind of trouble.

But the events of the past few days had insensibly wrought a change in her. She saw now that the sacrifice of her life would involve deep pain to another; and in the light of this new love a hundred doubts and fears, which had never troubled her before, now woke into active being.

Foremost amongst these was the haunting dread which Phil's warning had aroused. Would this man to whom she was pledged really give her back her word? Or had he been deceiving her?

She had never doubted Tor before, and she certainly need not have doubted him now; but if love brings with it a thousand bright hopes, it as certainly brings quite as many nervous fears.

Phil had unconsciously infected her with some of his own distrust of the man who passed as master of Ladywell, and she began to tremble lest he had deceived her, as the Signor said he had deceived others before. She tried to rid herself of these thoughts, she always spoke on behalf of 'Mr. Debenham' when he was attacked, yet the cold fear which had clutched at her heart would not relax its grip.

She had seen very little of Tor lately, which partly accounted for this change in her feelings. There was something straightforward and kindly in his presence, that always gave her confidence, and would have driven away her fears had she but seen him frequently face to face; but of late he had had much to occupy his time and thoughts, and he felt it well, under existing circumstances, to see but little of Roma.

True, not many days had passed since he had paid a hurried visit to her studio; but that did not count for much, and it seemed to her a long, long while since they had spoken together of their mutual understanding respecting their nominal engagement.

The girl's heart was heavy, and her face was pale when she met their guest at the breakfast-table upon the following day.

Phil saw this, and indignation waxed hot within him.

That morning Roma declined to allow him to enter her studio. She wanted, she said, to work hard, and should do so better alone.

Phil walked across the park to Ladywell, and wandered aimlessly about in its grounds and gardens, thinking bitter thoughts of his strange and anomalous position—a trespasser and an alien upon his own property.

He saw no one but a few gardeners, who looked curiously at him, but made no remark upon his presence there. He wandered at will amongst the flowers and shrubs, remarking to himself upon the beautiful order which reigned there, and wondering whether under his rule—if ever he obtained his own—things would be as well kept up.

'Tor always was made to rule—I used to tell him so: now perhaps he has found it out for himself, and has learned his own power.'

Phil was in a depressed frame of mind, restless and angry, yet still irresolute, from the feeling of helplessness which always came over him when he pictured himself standing up against Tor.

'He can turn me round his little finger,' said poor Phil dismally enough. 'He can do anything he likes with me, and he knows it. I believe if he had me to deal with, and only me, he could almost persuade me that I was Torwood, and he Debenham. I know the old feeling would all come back, and I should be like a child in his hands. I must have some help. I must make allies somehow. I wonder what these Belassis people are like. After all, they are my next of kin.'

Phil gathered a great bunch of roses and heliotrope for Roma, and then slowly turned his steps back to the house.

'My flowers!' he thought bitterly. 'I have to steal my own flowers, and run the risk of being prosecuted for it.'

No harm, however, resulted from his boldness. He met nobody as he retreated with his fragrant burden; only as he crossed the park, under the shadow of the great trees, he saw Maud and Tor riding gaily over the elastic sward up to the great terrace.

'What a handsome couple they are!' thought Phil. 'And how fond she is of him! I wonder what she will say when I have brought him to ignominy and disgrace. Will that steel her heart against me? I don't believe women have any sense of justice when their pity is aroused.'

He found Roma alone in the room, where the cloth was laid for lunch.

'Oh, how lovely!' she exclaimed, as she saw the flowers.

'For you,' he said softly. 'You know, Roma, what the heliotrope says?'

She bent her head over the flowers, and answered nothing.

'Tell me,' he said, with that gentle authority which a man in his position seldom assumes in vain.

'"*Ich liebe dich*,"' she answered so softly that he, too, had to bend towards her flowers to catch the words.

Next moment they had started apart, for Mr. Meredith had entered the room with a lady upon his arm, the sight of whose face made Phil start with surprise.

He knew at a glance who she was—his aunt, Mrs. Belassis.

Eighteen years had passed since he had seen her, but yet that handsome, cold face, with its hard lines and clearly cut features, had not been effaced from his recollection; and time had wrought little change in Mrs. Belassis.

Phil felt repelled by the face, though he tried not to let himself be too much led by his instinct of distrust. He had that gift of a somewhat finely strung nature, of reading faces with tolerable accuracy, and yet he did not wish to dislike or suspect Mrs. Belassis. She might prove a useful ally, and he was anxious not to allow prejudice to warp his judgment.

He talked with a purpose at table, and in a moment he saw that she understood and responded. It needed but a short time to convince him that Mrs. Belassis was a clever woman, and that she had some suspicions of her own respecting the character of her supposed nephew: though in what channel her suspicions ran, it was not the time and place then to discover.

Opportunity, however, was not long wanting, for an offer of escort home gave him the chance to speak to his aunt alone, and find out, if possible, what it was she really thought respecting Tor.

The interview was not entirely satisfactory, for, do what he would, Phil could not shake off the old distrust of his aunt; and the idea of plotting against Tor with a Belassis was so repugnant to all the instincts of his nature, that he could not bring himself to speak out plainly.

He saw that Mrs. Belassis was upon the wrong tack in her suspicions. She had no idea, as yet, of the trick that had been played upon the family; and Phil had, therefore, the acuteness to wonder how it was she so hated Tor, as to be willing to ally herself against him, and that with a perfect stranger. She must have a motive, and an interested one, else she would not trouble herself over the matter. What was it to her if Mr. Torwood was wronged? It was no business of hers to arbitrate between two friends.

So he plucked up his courage and put the question, and learned by the answer that Tor had treated with contumely his next of kin.

He could not help inwardly rejoicing that the Belassis faction had been so treated, for his soul abhorred them, even whilst his reason tried to persuade him into taking them into his confidence.

How he would have answered Mrs. Belassis he never had to decide; for as she finished her tirade against her ungrateful nephew, Tor himself came striding down the lane, and Phil felt himself crimsoning all over.

Suppose Tor could know him! Fancy such a juxtaposition! Phil in league with a Belassis against his old friend!

A sudden sense of shame fell upon him, as he met for an instant the keen, quick glance from Tor's eyes. There was no guilt, no shame in Tor's face; but the frank, open courage and truthfulness which had always characterized it.

No, come what might, he could not plot against his friend. He would speak to him openly, face to face. Phil's better angel was now in the ascendant, and he bid Mrs. Belassis a hasty adieu, whilst some words she had uttered, which had passed almost unnoticed before, now recurred to him with considerable significance.

'Spends Mr. Torwood's money almost more freely than his own,' he muttered in French; and then he added in vigorous English, 'The deuce he does!'

Phil pondered over this piece of intelligence a good deal. So Tor was spending his own money freely. Spending his own meant saving Phil's. If he was saving Phil's, what could be his object? Why should he save it, if he looked upon it as his own, and meant to claim it as such? Was it caution? or was it honesty? What could be the reason for economizing money supposed to be his own?

Phil puzzled over this question without solving the problem to his own satisfaction. On the whole, he inclined to believe that Tor was acting more fairly towards him than he had once believed; and yet he could not see his way out of the difficulty, nor understand how it was possible for his friend to be anything but false and treacherous.

He hung about Ladywell as a moth flits about a candle: it fascinated him to watch, as far as possible, the life that went on there; and yet the more he watched the more he saw how strong was Tor's position, and the more did he fear the result of trying to oust him.

'What would be the good to me of house and lands, if my sister hated me, and my aunt—the only aunt I care about—feared and blamed me? I should be detested at Ladywell, I know, if Tor were in prison. They will never love me as they do him. Maud is just wrapped up in him. Even Roma might turn against me then. Though she does not love him, she would pity him, and as everybody knows, pity is akin to love.'

It never occurred to Phil that Tor might be as much wrapped up in Maud, as Maud was in him, and the idea of his being in love with her never so much as entered his head. As he had been told that he was engaged to Roma, this was perhaps natural. As her heart was not concerned in the matter, his must be; otherwise the engagement could never have been formed.

The next event that followed was an invitation to dine at Ladywell.

This invitation Phil accepted readily. He was not now at all nervous of being detected, and his interest in that household was most absorbing.

Tor, in giving the invitation, had implied that it was merely a friendly dinner he was asked to share, that no company would be invited; and he thought that perhaps some opportunity would arise which would give him that private interview which he longed for whilst he dreaded.

When he reached the drawing-room he found two strange ladies there, as well as Maud and Mrs. Lorraine. One was a young girl of blooming countenance, the other a handsome, keen-eyed, well-dressed elderly lady, whose name was given as Miss Marjory Descartes.

Phil fancied the name was not altogether strange to him. He had a vague idea that he had heard it before, and that in some way or another it was associated with Tor; but he could not find the clue to the dim train of thought aroused, and as dinner was announced, his duty of conducting Maud to the head of her table now occupied his mind to the exclusion of all else.

Maud was very charming and very winning, of that there could be no doubt; and the more so from the little difficulties which arose in making herself understood to her neighbour. Her French was more broken and pretty than fluent, but her bright smiles and speaking gestures quite made up for lack of words; and Phil was more and more delighted with his sister, and more and more impatient to claim her as his own.

He noticed, even when in company and entertaining guests at her table, how her eyes were turning continually to Tor, how her face lighted when their glances met, and how she tried to catch what he said, and to include him in her own talk.

'How she does love him!' thought poor Phil. 'Will she ever love me like that? I should so hate to do anything to make her shrink from me. I will say nothing to-night, at any rate.'

This decision was a relief, and the short interval that he spent *tête-à-tête* with Tor, passed more easily than might have been expected. Phil concealed the nervousness he felt, and Tor seemed always at his ease. The interview did not last long, for they soon rose by mutual consent, to join the ladies.

Phil was glad to escape from his host, and fell readily into conversation with Miss Marjory Descartes, who attracted him by her bright, pleasant manner, and by her fluent, amusing speech.

But he was not altogether easy as the conversation proceeded. He could not define the impression produced; but he certainly experienced some sensation which suggested the idea that he was being 'turned inside out' for Miss Marjory's inspection.

If it was so, it was so cleverly done that he was barely conscious of the operation. It might be all his morbid fancy, he told himself. Miss Marjory could not by any chance know anything. Tor would know better than to betray his own secret. Still he could not be quite comfortable, and the more he reviewed the talk afterwards, the less he liked it.

He had committed himself, he feared, more than he had intended, and had not been clear as to his antecedents under cross-examination. He had come without a properly prepared story, and Miss Marjory had either found it out, or might have done so, if she had had any motive in her apparently innocent queries.

Miss Marjory had half fascinated, half frightened him.

He could not rid himself of the idea that she was in some way an ally of Tor's, and in his confidence. If so, it boded ill for him, for he knew that a clever woman was a dangerous enemy; and what Miss Marjory had said of Tor's likeness to Mr. Debenham and Maud seemed to imply that if an ally, she would be an unscrupulous one.

Such remarks as hers must have been made in all simplicity, or else with a deep motive. Phil was inclined to believe the latter theory; though at times he accused himself of morbid fears, which led him to suspect danger where no danger was.

Just at this juncture of affairs, came the invitation to join the dinner-party that was to celebrate Maud's majority. Michael Meredith, in his presumption that he and Roma almost belonged to the family, had all but asked for an invitation, and Tor had given it, including, as was almost necessary, the Signor.

At almost the last moment, after all, Meredith and his daughter decided against going, as his health was not considered strong enough to bear the fatigue. The Signor, however, to everyone's surprise, announced his intention of holding to his accepted word; and nobody exactly liked to say to him that his presence would be rather an intrusion. Roma had told him beforehand something about Mr. Debenham's odd will, and the decision Maud was expected to make. He was interested, but having no suspicions about the validity of the will, nor even of any compulsion put upon the father in its making, he did not attach the same significance to the matter that others had done.

Phil never forgot that dinner.

For the first time in his life he sat down to dine with a family party, and saw, for the first time since he had grown up, the three cousins he had played and quarrelled with as a child, and the uncle whom as a child he had so cordially hated. He did not now look in any way lovable. Phil could well believe that youthful impressions had been correct.

It was rather a terrible dinner for Phil. He could not disguise the interest with which he listened to the conversation that went on; and then Miss Marjory turned upon him, told him he was not an Italian, and asked why he could not say straight out who he was and what he had come for.

Phil had not a word to say, and for awhile sat dumb and confounded; but even a worm will turn, and he felt that he must do so. He tried to attack Miss Marjory, and find out what she did know; but he was defeated at all points. He was no match for his opponent; and all he could find out was, that he was known to be a spy, and, even if his identity was not guessed at, the object of his visit was; and that every means would be taken to defeat him, and to upset the claim he was about to put forward.

The enemy was even so strong that he was warned on his own account to desist, and plainly told that an attempt to coerce 'Mr. Debenham' would only recoil upon his own head.

Miss Marjory undertook to defeat him single-handed, and such was the respect inspired by her indomitable will and aggressive, confident manner, that Phil almost believed his cause already lost.

Like one in a dream he made his way to the library, where Maud's decision was to be heard. He resented Tor's attempt to exclude him as a personal affront. Who had the best right to be there, the brother, or the brother's friend?

Phil listened to all that passed with a feverish interest, not taking in its full significance, but observing only what he thought might be afterwards useful to himself. He saw that Tor had made bitter enemies of the Belassis', husband and wife, and knew that they would now support him, heart and soul, in his claim to wrest his own from the hand of their foe.

Very willingly did he now agree with Mrs. Belassis that the time had come to put an end to the game, and ready enough was he to meet her upon the morrow to discuss their campaign.

But then, again, when they had met face to face, he could not quite make up his mind to be frank. He despised the tools he had brought himself to employ, and was ready to hate himself for stooping to use them.

He did betray the secret, half unwittingly, and gave the clue of the tangle into his aunt's hands; but he let her believe that Philip Debenham was away at sea, for not yet was he prepared to give her his full confidence.

Their conversation has already been given; they nearly came to an understanding more than once; and then Phil, with instinctive distrust, pulled up, and would not commit himself further; but he knew that he had betrayed too much for it to be possible any longer to keep the game in his own hands;

and that, if his promise to Tor were to be redeemed, he must see and speak to him without delay.

He was to go to Ladywell as a guest next day. Nothing could be done before then, he thought, by Mrs. Belassis; yet, as he approached the door on his way to the Manor House, he encountered her coming forth.

'They *will* dispute it,' she said, in a hurried whisper. 'He means to keep the name and position he has assumed. Try your power if you will; but his mind is made up.'

Phil went slowly up to the house.

'I must try my power. I will. There is no other course open to me now. Whatever may be the result, I must make myself known. I will demand an interview this very night. I am glad that I cannot hesitate longer, that things have gone beyond my control. What will he say? How will he take it? Shame and fear and anger I must see, but oh! how strange they will look when stamped upon his face! Oh, Tor, Tor! why have you done this thing?'

CHAPTER VIII.
FACE TO FACE.

SIGNOR PAGLIADINI, on saying good-night to the company assembled at Ladywell, demanded a private interview with the master of the house.

Phil watched his host's face closely whilst he made known his wish, and saw that an expression of uneasiness passed over it, although Tor's manner was as frank and pleasant as possible.

He saw, too, a sharp look of inquiry in Miss Marjory's keen eyes, and felt more than ever convinced that this dangerous little woman was the confidante and accomplice of his former friend.

But every moment now was of value to him, and he could not linger to watch or think. He had a good ten minutes' start of his host, and he meant to make the most of it.

Dashing up to his own room, he locked the door, and flung off the dark, Italian-looking wig, leaving exposed to view his own dusky-brown hair, which was so like Maud's in colour and growth. Then out came a sharp razor, and after five minutes' rapid shaving the black, Vandyke beard had vanished, and the heavy moustache, with its long, pointed ends, was reduced to the ordinary dimensions accorded to Phil's.

Next, the padded coat was discarded, and an old blue smoking-jacket donned, which displayed the true proportions of the slightly-built figure. Some colourless fluid from a stoppered bottle removed a little of the intense blackness from eyebrows and moustache, and robbed the face and hands of some of their olive tinting; and Phil, glancing at himself in the glass, saw that, save for the slight swarthiness of complexion that could not be at once removed, his old self was entirely restored. The transformation was complete.

Then he unlocked the door, and waited with a beating heart for the arrival of his host. He could not decide how to meet him, nor what to say; he could not even think connectedly, so great was his excitement and agitation now that the supreme moment had come, when he and his false, treacherous friend should stand for the first time face to face.

There was a firm footfall outside, a hand was laid upon the handle of the door; Phil stood still in the middle of the room, and gave permission to enter.

The door opened.

'Now, Signor——'

There was a sudden pause, and for ten seconds utter silence reigned in the room.

'PHIL!' shouted Tor; and with one stride he had reached his friend and grasped him by both hands, in a strong, warm clasp that seemed as if it would never relax. 'Phil himself, by all that's wonderful! Phil it is, by the powers! though how you got here passes my comprehension! Phil, my dear old fellow, I can't tell you how thankful I am to see you. Oh, this is glorious!'

With an almost boyish gesture of delight Tor flung Phil's hands from him, and walked round and round him with a laugh of intense appreciation.

Phil stood aghast. He had pictured this meeting day by day for weeks, and never in the wildest flights of his imagination had he heard himself greeted thus.

Tor did not even observe his friend's silence in his own gladness of heart.

'Phil, you rascal, tell me how you came here? How did you escape from your vessel without my knowledge? I can't conceive how you came, but it's such an immense relief to have you back that I don't care for anything else. Did that Italian fellow smuggle you in? By-the-bye, where is he?'

Tor looked round him with a comical air of perplexity; and then, seeing the coat and wig lying on the bed, and the shaving apparatus upon the washstand, the true meaning of the situation dawned upon him.

He sprang upon Phil, and smacked him upon the back with all the force of his strong right arm.

'Phil, you scamp! you don't mean to say it was you all the time!'

And then he flung himself into a chair, and laughed till the tears stood in his eyes.

Phil stood gazing at him, feeling more and more like one who dreams, not knowing what to say, or what line of conduct to assume.

'You young villain!' cried Tor, as soon as he could speak, and he shook his fist at Phil with an expression that defies description. 'You young villain! you dare play me such a trick as that! You deserve to be hung, drawn, and quartered; and I'd string you up in two seconds if I weren't so glad to see you back. What have you got to say for yourself, you scamp!—worrying honest folks almost out of their senses with your dark sayings and sinister looks? And to think it was Phil Debenham all the time! Ye gods! What will Miss

Marjory say? I shall be a laughing-stock to her for evermore. Phil, you rascal, I'll never forgive you!'

And Tor laughed again more heartily than before; and after a long effort at dignified composure and coldness, old habit triumphed, and Phil's gravity gave way. He sat down opposite Tor and laughed with him until both were fairly tired.

'Tor, old man,' he said at last, 'I can't understand things yet; but it's borne in upon me that I've been a most infernal fool.'

'It's a way you have, dear boy, when left to your own devices,' answered Tor genially. 'I'd never have believed you could have played any game long, which I shouldn't detect; but how could I guess, when I believed you safe on board the *Medusa*? I can't make out how you did it, nor why. Phil, my boy, if you only knew how I've longed for you, and worried myself nearly into a fever, you'd never be able to say enough of my goodness and generosity! Why did you keep me a moment longer in such a position than was necessary? I should feel inclined to shake the life out of you, only this makes up for everything.'

'Tor,' said Phil, 'I've been such a consummate ass that I don't know how to tell you.'

'Let's come downstairs and smoke,' said Tor. 'I'm sure we shan't have done talking this side midnight. I'll mix some whisky punch, and we'll make a night of it. I'll do the honours of your house for this one night, old boy; and to-morrow, thank goodness, I'll resume my own personality and my humble name. Phil,' and he seized his friend's hand and shook it nearly off, 'you can't have a notion how glad I am to see you again!'

They went down to Tor's 'den.' On the way thither, Tor took the opportunity to slip a piece of folded paper under Miss Marjory's door.

The paper bore these words:

'It's all right. Phil has come back. Look out for larks to-morrow morning.— T. T.'

'What a comfort it is to sign one's own name again!' he thought, as he wrote the two T's.

'This is like old times,' said Tor, a quarter of an hour later, as the two sat together with pipes and punch. 'Well, Phil, how do you feel in your capacity as monarch of all you survey? Are you as glad to reign as I am to abdicate?'

'I may like it in time, when I don't feel such an egregious fool as I do now,' remarked Phil, as he smoked his pipe and looked at Tor, whose face expressed a sublime satisfaction.

'Well, what is it you've done?' asked the other. 'You'd better make a clean breast of it, as it seems so to weigh upon your mind.'

'Can't you guess?'

'I should be sorry to try. There are a vast variety of ways in which a man can make a fool of himself, and you always had a special aptitude in doing so.'

'Do be serious, Tor. You'll be serious enough when you hear.'

'Shall I? I don't feel overwhelmed with gravity so far. I can't get over the fact that you really made a fool of me, for once. To think that you and Signor Pagliadini were one and the same, and that you could meet me time after time, and I not find you out! I shall never be able to look Miss Marjory in the face again!'

And Tor broke anew into laughter.

'You're incorrigible, Tor!' cried Phil. 'I must tell you, if you can't see for yourself. I came in disguise because I was afraid to come otherwise.'

'Afraid!' laughed Tor; 'that's good. Afraid of what?'

'Of you.'

'Of me! Good heavens! why?'

'Now just be serious a moment, and put yourself in my place. I knew you had adopted my name, passed yourself off as my great-uncle's heir, and obtained possession of Ladywell. What could I think but that you intended to keep it?'

'Keep it!' shouted Tor; 'keep Ladywell! Be Phil Debenham all the rest of my natural life! No, thank you, my boy; not at any price! My dear old fellow, you never were very practical or very wise; but you don't mean to tell me you thought such a deception as that would be possible for any length of time?'

'I did,' said Phil. 'I suppose I was an ass for my pains. Perhaps my head was stupider than usual, but I thought it could be done, and that you could do it, if you had a mind.'

Tor opened his great grey eyes, and looked steadily at Phil.

'And did you think I had the mind?'

'What could I think? You had got possession of all that was mine. Why should you take it if you didn't mean to keep it?'

'Of course you couldn't understand why I should take such a step, without seeing some of the papers I must show you, now that you have come back;

- 70 -

but Phil, have we lived ten years together, and known each other since childhood, and have you so little confidence in me as that?'

Phil's eyes fell.

'I'm afraid I've been an awful fool—a fool and a brute both. I ought to have known.'

'Yes, Phil, you ought to have known. I'm not a saint, as you know, and I've never set up for being better than my fellow-men; but I don't think I've ever given you cause to think me a blackguard. Could you really believe in cold blood, that I should deliberately set about to rob you of your inheritance?'

'Old fellow, I'm awfully sorry. It must have been that sunstroke that muddled me. Don't be in a rage—don't cast me off. If you only knew how I feel now, you would see how much I am to be pitied.'

Tor smiled. He could not be angry with Phil—with the man who would always be a boy to him, whose oracle and king he had ever been, and whose allegiance could never be seriously shaken.

'You deserve a thorough good licking for being such a confounded muff; but you never do get your deserts in the way of chastisement. Phil, I have answered, and would answer, for your trust in me with my life; and *you* could believe this of me—you, my chosen companion and comrade—mine own familiar friend.'

'I have been punished,' said Phil slowly. 'I have not distrusted you without more pain than you can easily imagine. Can you forgive it and forget it?'

'To be sure. We will only think of the comic side of the question, for it is infinitely comic. After all, you had cause for bewilderment—only you might have trusted me. Come, Phil, tell me your tale. I can't still understand how you escaped without my hearing of it.'

So Phil told, graphically enough, the story of his awakening.

'The little wretch—so he played me false!' cried Tor, as Dr. Schneeberger's share in the conspiracy became known. 'I'd have sworn he was too deeply buried in the human brain to have risen to any kind of conspiracy. Why couldn't he have kept his word to me? I should like to punch his head so well, that his own brain should become an object of immediate solicitude.'

'Don't abuse him too much,' said Phil. 'He was loyal to you until I painted you so black that he couldn't well trust in you. When he was won over, he made a famous ally. It was he who devised the fiction of the sea-voyage, so as to account for my absence from his roof, should you chance to come over.'

Tor's eyes opened wide.

'Phil, you villain!' he said slowly, 'you don't mean to say you had come to your senses that last time I saw you in Germany?'

Phil looked at him, smiling deprecatingly.

'Well, that beats all! What a confounded ass you were not to have it out, then and there!'

'I would have done so, if you had only called me "Phil." Why did *you* keep up the fiction, Tor?'

'I—I like that! As if I could possibly be two people at once, or betray myself to anyone! As if I wasn't playing a risky enough game as it was, for the sake of your interests, without being expected to let others see what I was at. *I was* Phil Debenham when I went to Germany. You were Tor. A nice thing it would have been if I had gone and reversed positions!'

'But why were you Phil, and why was I Tor? and why were you so bold and defiant when I—Signor Pagliadini—told you that you were Torwood? It was enough to make anybody believe you meant to hold what you had got. Miss Marjory Descartes as good as told me that you would fight to the death.'

'Phil, you are a greater fool than I took you for! What else could I say or do until you came to claim your own? So long as you remained insensible and beyond my reach, I had to stick to my story like grim death; or I should have had the Belassis faction at my throat, and should have tasted all the sweets of prosecution for forgery and fraud.'

'Good heavens, Tor! What a risk you ran!'

'I did; and if I'd half realized the risk, I doubt if I should ever have run it, even for your sake.'

'For my sake!'

'Yes; you don't suppose I've put myself in a false position, and nearly got myself into a convict's cell, for my own amusement?'

'But what good could it do me?'

Tor rose, unlocked a drawer, and took out two letters: one from old Maynard, and one from Maud.

'Read those,' he said briefly; 'perhaps then you will understand better.'

Phil read in silence, and looked up at Tor for further enlightenment.

'Well?' he said.

'Well? Can't you see? These letters and the lawyer's, which you have seen, came whilst you were hopelessly insensible. Here was the lawyer, urging immediate return of the heir; Maud, begging and imploring her brother to come and release her from an uncongenial home. There were hints that Belassis was not to be trusted in the management of the estate, that you ought at once to come and take matters into your own hands. Then there was this marriage of Maud's to stop. You see how old Maynard wrote—and he wrote with sense as well as cynicism; and the important birthday was said to be imminent, though the date was not revealed. It seemed most urgent that some one should go over and look to things; and there were you, lying like a log, and with every probability of remaining in that state for weeks, perhaps for longer. You could not act yourself, you could not even empower me to act. If I had gone over as your friend, I should have had no power; and Belassis, as next of kin, lawyer, executor, guardian (under your father's will, I mean), would have had all his own way. For aught I knew, before you recovered, Maud would have been bullied into marrying his son; and you might have fallen so completely into his power, that he would serve you as he has served your father.'

Phil looked impressed and interested.

'You thought all that?'

'I did. You know what we have always said of Belassis between ourselves. I distrusted him then, though without the same ground, no less than I do now that I have had the honour of his acquaintance. I don't know what first put the notion into my head. It seemed to come all in a moment; and at first, I confess, my chief thought was that it would be a fine practical joke to play upon your people, just to personate you until you could come over and take up the *rôle* yourself. I knew nobody had seen you since you were a small boy, and I felt that I could play the part quite naturally and well for a few weeks, and rather enjoyed the idea of being the first to bring Belassis to see that his power had reached its zenith. I felt that that task would come easier to me than to you, old chap.'

Phil nodded.

'Go on. I begin to see.'

'I should hope you do. Well, I've about told you all now. Of course, once the irrevocable step taken, I began to see that it was something more than a joke; and I had to be very careful to leave no clue which could tell against me, in case a suspicion were raised. I believed every precaution had been taken, for that *you* would ever turn against me, never once entered my head, and even then I should not have thought you clever enough to overturn all my carefully laid plans. I had got on very well, on the whole, and weathered several threatened storms before you turned up; but, when you appeared, I knew there was danger ahead, and I sent for my only ally and confidante, Miss Marjory Descartes. I think she gave you a taste of her tongue on one or two occasions, did she not?'

'Yes, she scared me half out of my senses. Who is she, Tor?'

'An old friend of my father's—a very clever woman. You will like her, Phil.'

'If she doesn't make me nervous. How came you to confide in her, Tor?'

'I had to; she gave me no choice. She knew me from my likeness to my father; but I never regretted it; she has taken my part boldly.'

'She has. You ought to make her Mrs. Torwood.'

'I might do worse, if I were thirty years older; but, Phil, old fellow, my young affections are bespoken elsewhere.'

'I know.'

And poor Phil's face clouded suddenly.

'Do you? You have sharp eyes if you do. Think, Phil, what I have had to put up with for your sake—to pretend to be her brother all the time, and dispassionately to await her acceptance or rejection of other suitors. It's not many men who would have been so patient as I have been.'

'What are you talking about?' cried Phil eagerly. 'Whom is it you want to marry?'

'Maud—my sister up till to-night—your sister henceforward, thank goodness! Have you any objection?'

'Maud!' cried Phil ecstatically. 'Maud, is it? Oh, Tor, old fellow, what could be more to my mind? Oh, if I had only known! And I have been so madly jealous, thinking it was Roma!'

'Ah!' and Tor's eyes suddenly opened wide. 'So you and Roma have fallen a prey to one another, have you?'

'Yes, we understand one another; but she tells me, and her father tells me, she is engaged to you.'

'Roma knows that it is merely a fiction, our engagement, just to humour her father, who was very ill when he desired our betrothal—too ill to bear the irritation of a refusal. She could not explain this, but she knows it, and has, I hope, bestowed upon you the affections which certainly have never been mine. She will be glad enough, and so shall I, to be released from the bond. I am more tired than I can express of the continual fetter of a false position.'

'But Mr. Meredith——'

'He will not care, the old egotist! It was not me at all whom he wanted for his daughter; it was your father's son. He has always flattered his stupid old self that his will would bring about such a marriage. Now that you, the real son, have opportunely fallen in love with Roma, all will be well. He will transfer his affections, and those of his daughter, to you with perfect equanimity, and wonder the more at the magic power of his will. He is an old fool, but he is blind, and her father, so we must bear with him; but you need not fear opposition in that quarter.'

Phil drew a long breath of relief.

'Tor,' he said, 'yesterday I never thought I could be so happy as this again. If only I hadn't been such a brute as to doubt you!'

'Well, it's over now, and won't be likely to occur again; this makes up for all. Tomorrow, Phil, we'll go over the accounts together, and you'll see that I've not robbed you. I've spent a few hundreds of the money you were supposed to owe me, and a good deal of my own; but with yours I've merely kept the house going, and defrayed the expenses which you would have incurred in any case. I've quite turned into a business man, under stress of circumstances, and you'll find all as plain as a pikestaff. You'll never keep accounts like that yourself, my boy, not if you live till Doomsday. And now I can look the whole world in the face, and snap my fingers at the whole of the Belassis party. They're on the right scent now, and, but that we shall forestall them, might be nasty; but they are helpless so long as you stand by me, Phil, and say that all I have done has your sanction and approval. I suppose I may count on so much—eh, old boy?'

There was so much to say, now that the friends had once come together, so many jokes to enjoy together, so many episodes to laugh over, that it was two in the morning before they separated.

Phil's mercurial spirits had risen to the highest pitch of enjoyment.

'I say, Tor, we must have a lark out of this to-morrow.'

'All right. How?'

'I'm like Maud, am I not?'

'As like as two peas, and the image of your father, too.'

'Then introduce me at breakfast as your friend Mr. Torwood, and be Philip Debenham yourself, and see what they all say!'

'All right,' answered Tor, with a grin; 'I will.'

CHAPTER IX.
PHIL OR TOR?

THE following morning dawned bright and clear. Tor woke early, despite his late hours the previous evening, and woke with a joyous consciousness of being once more his own self—Torrington Torwood; no longer obliged to play a part, no longer obliged to watch his words and guard his conduct, and, above all, no longer forced to act towards Maud as if he were merely an affectionate brother.

With intense satisfaction Tor awoke to the fact that his task was done; and as he lay and considered the events of the past months, he thought to himself that, on the whole, it had been well done.

Things at Ladywell were on a very different footing now, from what they had been three months back. Then Mr. Belassis had had considerable influence in all affairs which concerned his nephew's property; he knew exactly what was done upon the estate, and how it was done. He had, during a brief period, managed all the buying and selling, and regulated the expenditure of the household and farms. Maud was all but engaged to marry his son, and did not attempt to deny that, had no strong hand held her back, she would most likely have pledged herself to do so.

Now, all idea of this marriage had been abandoned, and Mr. Belassis had gradually sunk into a very different position from the one he had formerly occupied in reference to the Ladywell property.

Firmly and quietly Tor had shelved his supposed uncle, and had gradually deprived him of every opportunity of tampering with his affairs.

He had not quarrelled with him, had not openly told him that he thought him a knave and a fool both; but he had conveyed to him in a hundred different forms the suggestion that he had much better mind his own business.

He had soon found that when he and the bailiff had the buying and selling to manage, the profits were much larger and the expenses less heavy. Belassis had been making a pretty profit out of the transactions he had carried on for three months, and was evidently hoping that his nephew would leave a good deal of responsibility in his hands still.

Phil might have done so, as Tor was fully aware. Phil was good-tempered, easy-going, and perfectly innocent of all malice or resentment. Anybody could get round Phil, who was a true Debenham in his dislike for 'a row' and his distaste for trouble; and any couple so unscrupulous as Mr. and Mrs. Belassis would soon have had him quite in their power.

'I don't think they can catch him now, though,' said Tor to himself. 'I've put them in their place, and they'll be obliged to stay there. Phil isn't a fool, though he's something of a muff in his laziness and good-nature; but I am pretty sure, after what I have to tell him, that he'll never have much to say to his precious relatives. And I think the Belassis' have too much sense to try to get round him, as long as I am on the spot, and that may be some time, unless Maud will have nothing to do with me;' and here Tor smiled to himself, as though he did not anticipate any very severe rebuff at Maud's hands.

When he was dressed he sought out Phil, who looked more than ever like himself, after another shave and a more vigorous attempt to remove his bronze.

Tor laughed aloud when he saw him.

'To think that yesterday you were that confounded Italian! Oh, Phil! I'll never forgive you for playing me such a shabby trick!'

'Now just hold your tongue, Phil Debenham,' laughed Phil. 'Don't you know I'm Mr. Torwood this morning, just returned from my travels—arrived late last night? There, let me brush my hair over my forehead. Don't I look just like Maud? Why don't you make love to me, Tor, old man?'

'Make love to an ass!' retorted Tor. 'Just part your hair decently, and come along. I've heard Maud and Miss Marjory go down. Don't snigger when you're introduced, or I won't go through with it.'

'All right,' answered Phil, beginning, nevertheless, to 'snigger' promptly. 'I'll be propriety itself. I don't promise not to grin when I see you kiss Maud, though!'

'If you do——'

'Oh, well, then I won't. Anything for a quiet life. Do come on. I want to see them all, and how they'll take it. Will Miss Marjory know?'

'Yes, but she won't spoil anyone's game. Come on.'

Two minutes later, Tor brought his guest into the breakfast-room. All the ladies were assembled there, some seated, some standing about, looking at their letters, and exchanging amiable remarks.

Maud sprang forward to greet Tor.

'Phil, you bad boy, you're late!' she said; and then she saw that he was followed by a stranger.

'My friend, Mr. Torwood, Maud!' said Tor, presenting Phil, who behaved very well, all things considered. 'He turned up late last night, and gave me no end of a surprise. You would give him a very warm welcome, if you half knew how glad I am to see him here.'

Maud turned to the stranger with her brightest smile, gave him her hand, and glanced into his face. Then the words of welcome seemed suddenly to die away. She looked at him, and then she looked at Tor, and back again at the new-comer, and she held her peace.

'Very glad to make your acquaintance, Miss Debenham,' said Phil, in a voice as exactly like her own as a man's can be like a woman's. 'My friend's relations almost seem to be mine.'

A warning look from Tor checked any further claim to relationship, otherwise he might have gone on from bad to worse.

Mrs. Lorraine had turned somewhat pale, and had sat gazing at Phil ever since he had entered, very much as one might gaze at one returned from the dead. She had not moved or spoken, nor did she seem capable of doing either.

Ethel was staring hard at Maud and the stranger, her round eyes full of astonishment.

Miss Marjory alone was equal to the occasion—as when was she not?

'Mr. Torwood!' she exclaimed, rising and advancing with her most gracious smile, 'this is an unexpected pleasure. Mr. Torwood, senior, was one of my best and most intimate friends, and I am delighted to make the acquaintance of the son, whom I have not seen since he was a baby in long-clothes.'

'He has grown a little since then, has he not?' said Phil, with his merry, mischievous smile (which made him more like Maud than ever), as he shook hands with Miss Marjory.

The ice thus broken, the remaining ladies were presented, and the party sat down to breakfast—Tor and Miss Marjory, as usual, making talk, to cover the unwonted silence of the others.

There was no mistaking the puzzled look on the faces round the table. Phil, of course, was all 'on the grin and the giggle,' as Maud afterwards described it, and was so bubbling over with secret amusement that it was all Tor could do to preserve a decent gravity, and address him in a natural way.

Mrs. Lorraine could do nothing but look at the stranger, and from him to Maud and back again; and her face wore an expression of bewildered perplexity that was almost pathetic.

Ethel's eyes were abnormally round; and Maud sat as if tongue-tied. She did not even wish to think; but she could not rid herself of the presentiment that some startling revelation was imminent.

'Where is Signor Pagliadini?' she asked presently, remembering for the first time their guest of the previous evening.

Phil sniggered audibly.

'He seems to have taken to himself the wings of the morning,' answered Tor readily. 'His room was empty as I came down. He's an odd chap. Perhaps he's off to Meredith's again. He's always doing something ridiculous.' Here he looked severely at Phil.

'I never thought Signor Pagliadini at all ridiculous,' observed Maud, by way of keeping up the conversation. 'He always seemed dignified and self-possessed.'

'So does a jackass at times,' returned Tor. Whereat Phil choked in a way which drew the eyes of the whole table upon him.

Tor felt that this state of things could not further be prolonged; but his instinct of mischief had been aroused, and he was determined to get what amusement he could out of the situation.

'What makes you stare so at Mr. Torwood, Maud?' he asked suddenly. 'You hardly ever seem to me to take your eyes off his face.'

Maud coloured vividly, and looked daggers at her wicked brother.

'Mademoiselle doubtless admires me greatly,' said Phil, with his Signor Pagliadini bow and smile. 'Mademoiselle flatters me more than I can say.'

Although he spoke English, there was something in tone and look so unmistakably identical with those of the supposed Italian, that an expression of utter mystification passed over all faces, save those of the two conspirators. Even Miss Marjory looked puzzled for a moment; but she quickly mastered the true bearing of past events, and laughed to herself heartily and silently.

Tor continued in his gravest way:

'Aunt Olive, you seem equally fascinated by my friend. His charms of person seem so to entrance you that you cannot even eat your breakfast. Tor, old man, I shan't be able to take you into society again, if you are going to cut me out like this.'

Phil's face quivered. He tried to answer, but failed signally, and, after several struggles to restrain himself, gave way and laughed irrepressively.

Maud sprang from her chair with flushed cheeks and dilated eyes. She made a sort of rush towards the man she had believed to be her brother, and then stopped suddenly short.

'Phil,' she said, in a trembling voice, 'what does it all mean?'

'What?'

'You know—you know quite well. Who is that man? and who are you?'

'"That man," as you forcibly describe him, is your brother, and my esteemed friend, Philip Debenham; and I, who by force of circumstances have heretofore been his *locum tenens* and representative, am now able to lay aside my borrowed plumes, and make myself known to you under my true name— Torrington Torwood.'

Phil had risen too, and was standing beside his sister.

'Maud,' he said softly, 'my own dear little sister, have you no word for me? You used to be fond of me, when we were little children playing together by the wishing-well. Our wish has come true—Ladywell is mine, but I shall not value it half so much as I do my sister's love.'

She knew him then, knew without a doubt that this man was her own brother; and with a sense of mingled sorrow, joy, and relief, she turned to him, and put her arms about his neck.

'Phil, dear Phil! It is you after all, then! Oh, Phil! what does it all mean?'

'It means that I have had the noblest, most generous friend that ever man did have. Maud, my little sister, you must love him for my sake and his own. We both owe very much to him.'

Phil had whispered these words as they stood close together, and the tumult of wondering voices drowned his low tones, which were only heard by Maud.

She knew well enough that what he said was true, and that to Tor's courage and independence of action they did owe very much.

He was not her brother at all; but she could not lose the sense of intimacy which the past three months had established between them. It was impossible all in a moment to realize that, in a manner, they were now strangers to one another.

She turned from Phil, who was at once folded in Aunt Olive's loving embrace, and faced Tor with one of her most bewitching looks—smiles, blushes, shyness and confidence all struggling together for mastery.

'I don't know what to say to you, sir, who have deceived us all these months; but I can't help being very glad you did, for I'm sure things would never have been so comfortably arranged if it had been Phil, not you, who had had the first settling to manage. I am ever so much obliged to you—Mr. Torwood.'

And she held out her hand, which he took, and kept possession of, whilst he looked long and smilingly into her downcast face.

'Thank you, Miss Debenham,' he said, releasing her; 'I am glad you have not cast me off altogether, in indignation at my deception. I have no intention of being cast off, I can tell you; and I shall lay claim to my privilege of a walk round the garden with you after breakfast, as usual.'

'Very well,' said Maud.

Her face suddenly crimsoned, and she hastily retired to her own seat behind the sheltering urn.

Her feelings were in such a tumult, that it was no wonder she desired to elude observation and give herself time to recover.

'But who and what was Signor Pagliadini?' cried Miss Marjory, when a little of the hubbub had subsided, and all had returned to their seats.

'Signora,' said Phil, in his polished Italian, 'you see now before you that misguided man, whom you so mercilessly frightened by trying to strip him of his disguise, before the time had come.'

'You Signor Pagliadini!' exclaimed Miss Marjory. 'Why, I shouldn't have thought you'd have the brains to play the part so well!'

'Exactly what my friend Tor told me. It's a great thing to have a faithful friend, isn't it? I see he has been faithful in his delineation of my character to you. It is gratifying to my vanity to have successfully deceived two such clever people.'

'You'd not have deceived me if I'd ever seen you as you are,' answered Miss Marjory stoutly.

'No, I don't believe I should,' Phil assented readily. 'Miss Marjory, you nearly frightened me into a fit at Maud's majority dinner,'

'I wish I'd frightened you more,' returned she viciously. 'You've not got half what you deserve, practising on the credulity of honest people, and making us all so uncomfortable. What did you do it for?'

'Because I was an ass—a dignified jackass, as Tor has so aptly described me. I can't resent the description, because it's true to the life. I'll tell you all about it soon; but let me enjoy myself now.'

'The dear boy!' murmured Mrs. Lorraine tenderly. 'The dear, dear boy! So like his father! Poor dear Philip—if only he could have lived to see this day!'

'Aunt Olive, you've not changed a bit,' cried Phil. 'You're just as pretty as ever. Do you remember how I used to upset your workbasket every day, and tell you not to mind, because I'd marry you when I'd grown as big as you?'

'Bless you, I remember it like yesterday,' answered Mrs. Lorraine, with tears in her eyes.

'I'm so sorry the old house has gone. I should have liked to have seen the little octagon room again, where you used to sit and work, Aunt Olive. I slept in the room over it, I know, and liked it so much because it had the evening and morning sun, both. Do you remember the big griffin I drew on the wall to frighten Maud? And how frightened I was myself because it wouldn't rub out, and always seemed grinning at me in the dark? You papered the room with rosebuds yourself, then, you dear old auntie, to save me from a scolding from papa.'

There was certainly no mistaking the real Phil when once he had come. He was full of reminiscences of former places and old friends. Tor had done well with what slight knowledge he possessed of Phil's childhood; but the real Phil could go on by the hour with boyish recollections of Ladywell and home.

Maud escaped to the garden when the breakfast-party rose. Just at present she could not talk freely to the newly-found brother; she was too much startled and perplexed by the suddenness of the change.

It had been a habit from the first, that she and Tor should stroll round the garden together before the day's work began; and from what he had said, she fancied that he intended still to keep up this habit. How would he treat her now? how would he behave? He had always been so quiet and reserved in his affection, she so open and familiar.

She felt glad now that he had acted thus, for she saw that he had taken no undue advantage of his position, and respected him the more for it; but she did wish (and her cheek crimsoned at the thought) that she had herself been a little more reserved in the affection she had expressed for himself.

'But it wasn't my fault,' she said to herself, half aloud; 'for I thought he was my brother, and I did love him ever so much.'

'Don't put it into the past tense, Maud,' said a voice behind her; and she found that her hands were held fast by Tor. 'Is a brother the only person in the world you can love?'

Maud's eyes fell before his, but she did not try to withdraw her hands.

'Have you transferred *all* the love you had for me to the real Phil?' he asked again.

'I suppose I ought,' answered Maud, beginning to smile. 'I suppose in time I shall; but, you know, you have told me that transfers are tedious and tiresome affairs.'

'So they are, Maud,' he answered—'much too tedious and tiresome to be worth the undertaking in some cases. Look here—let me help you out of a difficulty. Give Phil as much love as ever you like—new love for the new Phil, and let me keep the old love that I have won. It was not *all* given to me, was it, Maud, because I was thought to be a brother?'

He drew her towards him, and she did not resist, not even when her head was touching his shoulder.

'You love me, Maud?'

'You know I do. I'm sure I've told you so often enough. It's no good going on in the proper way and pretending I don't,' said poor Maud, who felt that her maiden's privilege of fibbing was taken away from her by force of circumstances.

'I have loved you ever since I knew you. You don't know how hard it has been to call you "sister."'

Maud nestled more comfortably against his shoulder then.

'You dear boy! Are you sure?'

'Quite sure. I've had a few youthful spoons, Maud. I won't lie to you, even in a moment like this. But I've never really loved a woman till I loved you; and I feel as if I could love as well as most men. You shall be the one to prove if it is not so.'

'You dear boy!' said Maud again.

'Sometimes you've complained that I haven't kissed you often enough, Maud. If you don't mind, I'll make up for the deficiency now.'

Maud did not seem to mind at all. She turned up a happy face, which was certainly well kissed.

'I'm glad you're not my brother, Tor,' said Maud, when the kissing was over.

'So am I,' he answered gravely. 'This is much more satisfactory, isn't it?'

'Very much more,' she answered; and by-and-by she added, 'and Tor's a much nicer name than Phil. Phil doesn't suit you: it sounds too small. I wonder I never thought of it before.'

'If we stay here much longer, we shall have other people upon us,' remarked Tor.

'Let us go, then, and hide,' cried Maud eagerly. 'We've got such lots to say.'

'Haven't you lots to say to Phil?'

'Oh, Phil can wait!'

Not displeased at this sentiment, Tor led Maud away to a secluded part of the park, where they passed a couple of hours in a fashion infinitely satisfactory to themselves, but not interesting to the historian.

They were soon missed by those that remained; but Phil and Miss Marjory only smiled, and said they had better not be sought for.

Phil told his story to her, and received a good deal of the verbal castigation for which Miss Marjory was famous.

'Not trust Mr. Torwood! You who had known him eighteen years! I never heard anything so disgraceful in my life! You ought to be ashamed of yourself! I knew he was to be trusted before I had known him eighteen hours.'

'We cannot all be so clever as you, Miss Marjory.'

'Now——' she began warningly; and Phil was silenced, though not for long.

'Don't hate me, Miss Marjory, please.'

'I don't think you're worth hating.'

'No, I'm not—I assure you I'm not. You've just hit the mark. I'm not worth your lofty scorn and contempt, so please reserve it for a more deserving object.'

And then Miss Marjory laughed, and she and Phil made friends.

'Ah, my dear,' she said, an hour or two later, as she met Maud dancing and singing along the corridor, 'didn't I give you good advice, when I told you that you had better wait for Mr. Torwood?'

'You did indeed, Miss Marjory.'

'Was I very wrong in asserting that he might possibly resemble the adored "Phil"?'

Maud kissed her suddenly on both cheeks.

'You were right, as you always are—a real fairy godmother; and I was a very good child, and did exactly as you advised!'

CHAPTER X.
MR. AND MRS. BELASSIS.

I THINK I must take you over to Thornton House this afternoon, Phil,' said Tor, 'and reintroduce you to your esteemed aunt and uncle.'

Phil made a grimace, which indicated that he did not look forward with eagerness to the impending introduction to his kinsfolk.

'I wanted to go and see old Meredith.'

'We'll take him on the way back, if you like,' answered Tor; 'but you ought to go first to see the Belassis family.'

They were sitting at lunch when this conversation took place, and Phil, for the first time, had taken his place at the foot of the table. Tor sat beside Maud, and seemed to feel in nowise degraded.

The servants knew nothing of the transformation which had taken place. They believed that the young squire had arrived late the previous evening, and that the Signor had been called away the following morning. They were too much excited by the sudden change of master to have much interest to spare for the Italian.

All their thoughts were given to puzzling over the strange change which had taken place; and all tongues were uttering speculations as to why Mr. Debenham had sent Mr. Torwood in his place, and made him take his name for three whole months.

Phil was glad enough that it should be so. He was heartily ashamed of his distrust of his friend, and consequently the whole of the Signor Pagliadini episode was highly distasteful to him. He felt degraded by the thought that he had come in disguise to spy upon Tor; and he was really anxious that the matter should remain unknown, outside the walls of his own house.

Hence his reluctance to face Mrs. Belassis.

'I was almost conspiring with her against Tor,' he said ruefully. 'I could not bear her ever to remind me of that, and I know she will.'

'Why should she ever have the opportunity?' said Miss Marjory. 'It will be your fault if she does.'

'How?'

'It was Signor Pagliadini, not Mr. Philip Debenham, who nearly made a confidante of her.'

Miss Marjory spoke with some significance, and Phil's face brightened.

'You think I needn't say that I was the Signor?'

'Why should you say so?'

'I don't know, I'm sure. I fancied it would all have to come out.'

'Why?'

'I don't know. Don't you think she'll suspect?'

'No, I don't—I'm quite sure she won't,' said Miss Marjory, nodding her head emphatically. 'If you deceived me, young man, I'm quite sure you equally deceived Mrs. Belassis.'

'I think,' said Mrs. Lorraine gently, 'that no one besides our six selves need ever know exactly how matters really stand, or that Mr. Torwood ever acted as anything but dear Philip's deputy.'

'Quite so,' said Miss Marjory. 'Mr. Torwood was doing the best thing possible for his friend's interests; and if not very wisely, he acted most generously, and great good has been done by it.'

'Indeed, yes,' cried Phil eagerly; 'and do you really think nobody else need know what an ass I've been?'

'If you don't betray yourself,' said Miss Marjory, 'nobody else will betray you.'

Phil drew a long breath of satisfaction.

'Oh, jolly!' he cried in his boyish way; 'and won't my uncle and aunt be sold! They'll think I knew all the time that Tor was here, and that I was in the plot. I hope they will feel properly "done."'

'You must be bold and firm with them,' said Miss Marjory; 'you must stand up for every measure your friend has taken. You must say that everything he did has your complete sanction.'

'Of course I shall.'

'And they can easily be made to believe that you were aware the whole time of your friend's movements.'

'And they shall think so too!' cried Phil eagerly; 'and if they try to cast in my teeth what that old Pagliadini said, I will lay it hot on him!'

'I think you will enjoy abusing the Signor,' remarked Maud, smiling.

'That I shall,' cried Phil. 'I abuse him to myself every time I think of him.'

'Well,' said Tor, bringing matters round to the point from which they had strayed, 'is it agreed that we call together at Thornton House to-day?'

'It is,' said Phil.

At Thornton House that day a somewhat animated interview was taking place between Mrs. Belassis and her husband.

It will doubtless be remembered that it was only upon the previous afternoon Mrs. Belassis had made an attack upon Tor at Ladywell, and had heard from Miss Marjory the disgraceful story of her husband's first marriage, and his subsequent desertion of his young wife.

She had appeared to take the news quietly, for she had not been able, in her excitement and indignation against Tor, to consider with calmness her own possible position; and she had, at the moment, felt convinced that the first wife must have died, and that he must have known of her death before he had dared to marry again; but when she began to review the subject dispassionately, a great fear fell upon her that this might not be so, and a hundred little forgotten incidents rose up before her, all tending to increase her doubts. Her husband's eagerness to engage himself to her, and his constant postponement of the wedding, looked significant enough to her now. His ill-assured manner all through the marriage day and later, and his wish not to advertise the ceremony, came back to her memory now and made her tremble. Then his fear and anxiety when Whitbury was named were certainly strange, as was also his craven and cowed air when he had met Miss Marjory.

It was possible, of course, that he might be cowed and timid, in any case, at meeting one who could reveal the fact of the first marriage; but all seemed to point to the conclusion that he had never really ascertained the fate of the woman he had wedded only to desert.

Mrs. Belassis could not speak to her husband on her return, for he had started upon a business expedition from which he was not expected home until the following day.

Time, however, gave Mrs. Belassis opportunity to nurse her wrath and plan out a course of action, and certainly the expression of her countenance, as she sat at the luncheon-table opposite the husband, who had just returned, boded him no good; and after one or two feeble attempts at conversation, he sank into silence, quaking inwardly and wondering what was to come.

'I wish to speak to you, Mr. Belassis,' she said, as they rose from table.

'Certainly, my love.'

Lewis and the girls looked on aghast. The latter had felt that a storm was brewing, and had not dared to tell their father and brother, as they were longing to do, that 'Phil' was engaged to Roma, and that he was not really 'Phil' at all, but an impostor.

They had felt bound to keep silence at luncheon; but when their father and mother had retired to the study, they pounced upon Lewis and poured into his ears the bewildering tale which they had lately heard themselves.

Mr. Belassis followed his wife slowly and reluctantly into his study, feeling that an evil time lay before him.

'Sit down, Mr. Belassis,' she said.

He sat down meekly.

'Well, my love, what is it?'

'Don't call me "my love" again, until I give you leave. What has become, Mr. Belassis, of your first wife? Tell me that.'

'My—f-first—wife!'

'Yes, your first wife—you are not going to look me in the face and say you have not had one!'

He did not look her in the face, and he did not utter a word.

'Where is the first Mrs. Belassis—tell me that!'

'Dead.'

'Are you sure?'

'Y-yes—I'm as sure as I can be.'

Mrs. Belassis shivered slightly. It was, then, as she had suspected.

'When did she die?'

There was a pause; which he broke by answering with assumed assurance:

'Ages ago; long before I married you.'

'That's a lie!'

He shrank before her tone and look.

'How—how do you know?'

'I know that she was alive three months before you married me.'

His face turned livid.

'How do you know?'

'I was told, on good authority.'

'By whom?'

'By Miss Marjory Descartes.'

'Good heavens!' cried the miserable man, starting up. 'If you've been talking to her, it's all over with me. She has no mercy.'

Then there was a long pause, which at first neither seemed inclined to break.

'You mean to tell me, then,' said Mrs. Belassis, at last, 'that I am not your wife at all?'

'I don't know,' he cried desperately. 'I can't tell you anything—I don't know myself. I never could find out what became of her. I did make inquiries—I did all I could. I found out that she had left Whitbury, that she was in a consumption, and was gone away south, and was not likely to live through the winter. I couldn't get to know where she was, and you wouldn't wait longer. I made sure she had died in the winter, and I believe still that she did; but I don't know, and I can't say more.'

Mrs. Belassis looked coldly and scornfully at him.

'I wouldn't wait! Hadn't I waited five years for your whims? Was it likely I cared for you enough to waste my whole life waiting? Why didn't you tell me you were a married man?'

'I didn't know whether I was or not,' he answered sullenly.

'Then why didn't you say that you didn't know?'

He glared at her like a wild beast at bay.

'Take care, Mrs. Belassis—take care! Don't drive me too far.'

'I am not aware that I am Mrs. Belassis.'

'You're not aware that you're not, anyhow. I believe you are; and when I've proved this miserable creature's death, I'll make you feel that I am your lord and master.'

Some of the old brutal power of the man was returning to him in this extremity. There had been a time when Mrs. Belassis had half-feared and admired, whilst she half-despised him. It seemed as though danger of disgrace had roused in him some of his old force of character.

'You'd better not threaten me, Mr. Belassis. So long as the doubt remains a doubt, I will stay where I am, and act as your wife; but remember, that whether or not our marriage is legal, you have behaved abominably; and if I expose you, you will not find it pleasant.'

'It will hurt you more than it hurts me—exposure will!' began Belassis savagely; then, catching the look in her eye, he paused and said: 'Come, Celia, be reasonable. What is the good of our quarrelling? Nobody need know this miserable story, unless you betray it; and they'll find it hard to prove that *she* was alive, as nobody seems to know where she went to, when she left Yorkshire. I don't see that anybody can have any interest in raking up an old story like that; and I shall be always ready to swear to her death. I'll get a certificate if necessary. I can easily manage that.'

Mrs. Belassis sat silent.

'*I* must know the truth. I cannot go on like this,' she said slowly. 'But so long as matters remain uncertain, I suppose things must go on as they are. We have one enemy, however, who knows of the existence of the first Mrs. Belassis, and of the doubt of her death. He will ruin us if he can!'

'Who is he?'

'The man now calling himself Philip Debenham and our nephew.'

'Calling himself?'

'Yes; that man is really Torrington Torwood!'

'Celia!'

'He is. I have suspected him for long. I knew all was not well, though I could not lay my finger on the fraud. I know, now, what it is—the man is an impostor—only that!—an impostor and a forger!'

'How do you know?'

'Signor Pagliadini told me.'

'That Italian? Does he know Philip and his friend?'

'He has known them both well. It is Mr. Torwood who is reigning here. Poor Philip is in a kind of captivity, awaiting his tyrant's orders. At present he is at sea—safely out of the way.'

'We must rescue him!' cried Belassis, a vision of golden possibilities rising at once before his eyes. 'We, his next of kin, will rescue him from the clutch of this villain, and reinstate him in his own inheritance! Celia, my love! the tables will be turned, and our fortunes will be made! We will drive out this impostor with scorn and obloquy! I will prosecute him myself, and he shall be transported for life! Penal servitude is just fit for him, and such as he! When dear Philip has his own again—ah, how different it will all be! I knew that man was not a Debenham, and Philip must be his father's own son, or this Torwood could not ride rough-shod over him as he does. Ah, my dear! when we get our own nephew safe under our protection at Ladywell, how different everything will look!'

This had been Mrs. Belassis' own conclusion, but she saw more difficulties in the way.

'We must prove our case first. Torwood will not give way readily. I charged him with the fraud yesterday, openly, but he had the impudence to look me in the face and tell me that he should prefer to hear of such matters through my legal adviser! Oh, you needn't be afraid! He's Torwood, as sure as you're Belassis; but he has got the property, and he will fight for it.'

Belassis considered awhile, and his eye began to glitter.

'So much the better, perhaps. Phil's gratitude will be all the greater, after a hard fight.'

'We must find Phil first.'

'True. Does anyone but this impostor know where he is?'

'I fancy Signor Pagliadini does.'

'Who is this Signor Pagliadini?'

'I don't know. Evidently some friend of Phil's, who has come over to look after his interests.'

'Has Phil sent him?'

'I don't know. He cannot speak English, and he is very reserved about himself.'

'But he is Torwood's enemy?'

'I should say so.'

'And therefore our friend.'

'Don't be too sure of that. He was anything but open with me. I wormed a good deal out of him; but I'm not sure that he intended me to.'

'We'll make him speak out!' cried Belassis heartily and eagerly. 'I've not been a lawyer for nothing; and I flatter myself I know how to get at information when I want it, and how to get up a case when I've an object to gain. The first thing to do, when we've won over this Signor, is to find our poor wronged nephew; and the next, to prosecute this Torrington Torwood for forgery and fraud.'

A knock at the door had passed unheeded, so it was simply thrown open, whilst the servant briefly announced:

'Mr. Debenham and Mr. Torwood.'

Dead silence reigned in the room, as the two young men made their entrance.

'Good-afternoon,' said Tor pleasantly. 'I hope we do not interrupt anything very important. I felt I must not lose time in introducing to you your real nephew, Philip Debenham, or in explaining to Mrs. Belassis that her shrewd surmise as to my identity is perfectly correct. Yesterday the time had not come to declare it; but now it has, and I have great pleasure in withdrawing from the position I have hitherto held as your nephew, and in presenting the rightful claimant for your affections, Philip Debenham.'

If a bomb had exploded in their midst, it could not have produced a more profound sensation of dismay and consternation.

'You seem surprised, uncle,' said Phil, advancing with a smile. 'I should have thought you would have been prepared by my aunt.'

'My dear, *dear* boy!' stammered Belassis, with all the fervour his confused mind could muster. 'My own dear Philip! welcome, welcome home to your true friends, who really care for you and your interests!'

'Well, uncle, I'm glad enough to get home,' said Phil. 'It's not been my fault I've stayed away so long; and for the rest, this friend here has looked so well after me and my interests for the past ten years, and especially for the past three months, that I can't say I feel any special yearnings after new ones.'

Mrs. Belassis was gazing coldly and fixedly at Tor, who seemed quite at his ease even under the awful glare of her eyes.

'Young man,' she said threateningly, 'do you imagine for a moment that you will be allowed to escape all the consequences of this gross imposition and fraud, which you have been practising upon us?'

'I'll take my chance of that,' answered Tor serenely. 'I don't feel under any pressing anxiety, so far.'

'We shall prosecute,' said Mrs. Belassis grandly.

'I shall be delighted if you do,' answered Tor. 'I'm afraid you will find some difficulty in procuring counsel.'

'Difficulty!'

'Well, it's generally rather difficult to get counsel when you've got no case,' explained Tor affably.

Mrs. Belassis was silent, through extreme indignation. Her husband, who better understood the law, appealed with more zeal than discretion to his nephew.

'You must prosecute. Philip! You must not let this act pass unnoticed and unpunished. He has signed your cheques and papers, and perpetrated every kind of fraud. You must not allow such a monstrous imposition to go unpunished—for the sake of justice you must not.'

'Well, sir, I think justice can take care of herself without any protection from me; and as for prosecuting Tor, for doing me the greatest service in his power, I never heard of anything so monstrously ridiculous in all my life.'

'The greatest service!' echoed Mrs. Belassis. 'A service to rob you of your name, get your affairs into a shocking state, and quarrel with all your friends. Fine service, indeed!'

'Yes, a great service. I was ill—I could not attend to things myself; but he has brought everything round to a most satisfactory issue. My agent did much better than I could have done.'

'Your agent! He did not come as your agent, but as yourself.'

'Exactly—the only satisfactory way in which he could come. Why he did so, is his business and mine. You had better not inquire more closely into the matter.'

'Your agent! Signor Pagliadini said——'

'Signor Pagliadini is an old fool.'

'You know him, then?'

'Yes, for a meddling, blunder-headed fool. You will see no more of the Signor, Aunt Belassis.'

'Has he gone, then?'

'Gone to the place he came from, to hide his diminished head. He vanished double-quick, I can tell you, when I appeared upon the scene.'

This was the final blow. All lingering hope of proving Tor a villain, was crushed by the news of Signor Pagliadini's sudden flight.

'Well, I don't think I'll stay longer to-day,' said Phil. 'You seem altogether too much astonished to have anything to say. I'll look in another day when you have got over your surprise. Tor would have me come to report myself at headquarters, and I've done it now. You may congratulate yourself, uncle, that you had Tor to deal with in the first place, not me. I'm an awful duffer at business, and never do understand things. Any fool could cheat me. But Tor, he's made of different stuff, and he can't have tried your patience half so much as I should have done. You'll be saved all trouble now with my stupidity, for he will teach me everything. He's so well up in all my affairs, that I feel as if he ought to be the master.'

So Phil and Tor departed, leaving the husband and wife alone together.

They looked in silence into each other's faces, as if they both felt that a great calamity had befallen them.

'Can we not prosecute, then?' said she.

'Impossible, so long as Philip supports him.'

'It's a disgraceful scandal!' said the wife.

'It is,' assented the husband. 'Oh, what a monstrous shame it has all been! If only we had had that other man to deal with, all would have been safe, and Maud would have been Lewis's wife by this time. He is the very image of his father. I could have turned him round my little finger.'

'It seems to me that we are pretty nearly ruined every way,' said Mrs. Belassis; 'and we shall be most certainly, if that will in the Ladywell library is ever found. Five thousand you can pay, and the interest we claim as recompense for Maud's expenses whilst under our care. But fifteen thousand with interest for eighteen years——'

'Would mean simple ruin. The trust-money is all gone.'

'I know it, and we must find the will,' said Mrs. Belassis; 'though I don't know if there is any reason why I should trouble myself over your affairs now.'

CHAPTER XI.
MR. MEREDITH S VIEW.

THINK I gave him one that time,' said Phil, as they walked away. 'How I hated him, when I saw him again!—just as I did when I was a small boy and he bullied me.'

'They are mad that they can't prosecute me,' said Tor, laughing. 'I should get scant mercy at their hands.'

'He looks a regular old scoundrel, and I believe he is one; but I don't believe I should dare to defy him, if I hadn't you at my back.'

'The old story—eh, Phil?'

'It will be the old story till the end of the chapter, I expect, old man. You mustn't desert me when you marry Maud.'

'No fear.'

'I shall do as old Maynard wished, and make good the money to her; he would have left it to her, if he hadn't been afraid of doing more harm than good.'

'Well, it's not for me to stand in the way of what you think right; but I have plenty for both, you know, and Ladywell wants keeping up.'

'Maud shall be well dowered, anyway—that's my positive duty as head of the family; but is there no way of punishing that Belassis for ruining my father, and destroying his last will?—for I know he did both.'

'We can't prove even the existence of that other will, much less its destruction, though we are quite convinced of both. As to the other question, I have made out that it would be a difficult matter to open an inquiry at this distance of time. Besides, you know, a knave can ruin an honest man without going beyond the limit of the law, if he only knows how to set about it. I believe Belassis did know that well.'

'The old scoundrel!' muttered Phil. 'I wish we could ruin him.'

'Strikes me he'll ruin himself some of these days, without any assistance from us.'

'How so?'

'Speculation.'

'Ah! you think that?'

'I do; and it strikes me it will be all he can do to produce the £5000 of Maud's trust-money, which will have to be handed over.'

'You don't mean to say you think he's played fast and loose with that?'

'I do. I am pretty sure it is so, otherwise he would have cared little about the marriage. It is either that, or else the fear that the later will may turn up—if he has not found and destroyed it.'

'The old scoundrel! Come, Tor, we'll change the subject, or I shall lose my temper. Shall we go to the Merediths' now?'

'If you like.'

'I do like. I want to get things settled with Roma. Tor, old man, you'll settle the father for me, won't you?'

'All right; but you must come too, or he'll not believe me when I try to explain.'

'He won't have a fit or anything, I hope?'

'Oh no! He'll not care a bit, so long as Philip Debenham is willing to marry his daughter.'

'He's an old ass!'

'Don't tell Roma so, anyhow; and don't be so free of your opinions respecting your future father-in-law.'

Phil felt slightly rebuked, more by the tone than the words.

'It's only to you, Tor. I rather like the old boy, really.'

'He's not bad, if he can once be made to forget himself.'

'Roma is an angel! I never knew so devoted a daughter.'

'I don't think her life has been a happy one heretofore; mind you make it more so, Phil. She has very warm feelings, as I dare say you know better than I, and the passionate nature of the South, little as one would think it. Her father's blindness was caused by her, in a fit of fury. She will tell you the story herself, no doubt; she was more sinned against than sinning, I shall always say. I don't think she has ever got over the shock and the grief, and it seems to have crushed out all the passion of her nature, and almost all else but the devotion to her father. Remember that, Phil; and be very gentle and patient if she does not all at once yield to you the first place, which naturally seems your right.'

'I will, my Mentor; I will! Give me all the good advice you can, for I'm a muff, and I know it; but I do love Roma!'

'Then love will teach you better than I,' said Tor; and they walked on in silence.

'Ah, Philip Debenham!' said Michael Meredith, as the two entered the room together. 'Philip Debenham and my friend the Signor. I am happy to welcome you both.'

'You will welcome one of us still more warmly, when I have introduced him afresh,' answered Tor, as he took the old man's hand in his.

'You are pleased to speak in riddles, Philip,' said Meredith, smiling.

'Not at all, sir, I assure you.'

'Do you mean to say that I require a new introduction to my friend Signor Pagliadini?'

'I do indeed!'

Meredith was smiling blandly, as if he rather enjoyed the little mystery.

'Under a new name?'

'Yes; a new name that is yet not altogether new to you.'

'Then let me hear this new, familiar name.'

'The name of my friend here,' said Tor quietly, 'is Philip Debenham!'

'Very much at your service, sir,' said Phil, in his own voice and tongue; 'who has to return you many thanks for your hospitality, and begs to apologize for the deception practised upon you.'

Michael Meredith had started, and changed colour somewhat, as Phil's voice had fallen upon his ear.

'Philip Debenham! Philip Debenham!' he repeated slowly. 'It is, indeed, as if one had returned from the dead! It is the voice of my well-beloved friend himself!'

'Of his son, at least, Mr. Meredith, who hopes soon to become well beloved on his own account,' said Phil.

'But you, Philip—I mean, you whom I have learned to call Philip, in spite of early misgivings—who and what are you?'

'Philip no longer, now that my work of deputy is done. I assure you, Mr. Meredith, I have acted in all things merely as a deputy.'

'And who are you, then?'

'He's the best fellow in all the world!' cried Phil impulsively; 'my friend Torwood!'

'You are Philip Debenham—there can be no doubt of that!' said Meredith slowly; 'but why was this mystery made? Why were you represented by your friend? Why did you appear here in disguise? And how did you obtain an introduction from my esteemed relative Signor Mattei?'

Tor explained the matter briefly and clearly, as much, at least, as there was any need to explain. Mr. Meredith listened with interest and attention. He seemed amused and entertained by what he heard, which had about it a flavour of romance that just suited him. He was quite ready to become an accomplice, and promised never to reveal the fact that Phil and the Signor were one and the same. He was not likely to publish anything which should show that his perceptions had ever been at fault.

Suddenly, however, a cloud seemed to settle upon his brow. Tor saw it, and understood its meaning, and signed to Phil to depart.

Phil obeyed gladly, being all on fire to find and claim Roma as his own.

'Now, Mr. Meredith,' said Tor, when he and the old man were alone together, 'you and I have a little matter to discuss between us.'

'Yes, Mr. Torwood; and I am a man of honour. If I must keep my word, I must; but this has been a shock to me.'

'In what way, sir?'

'Can you not guess?'

'Perhaps you are thinking of your daughter?'

'I am. I have liked you, as you know, for your own sake. I would gladly welcome you as a son-in-law—and yet—I have set my heart upon marrying Roma to Philip Debenham's son.'

'And you may do so still! Have I not said that *in all things* I have acted merely as my friend's deputy?'

Meredith's face expressed a sort of surprised satisfaction.

'Engaged yourself to Roma by deputy, do you mean, Mr. Torwood?'

'I think, sir,' said Tor, smiling, 'that it was you who engaged us. We had little voice in the matter, if you remember.'

'Ah, well, I may have said the most; but I quite understood that you accepted.'

'I did not decline, because it would have hurt you if I had done so at such a moment; and besides, I had no right.'

'How so?'

'It was not to me, but to my friend Philip that the proposition was made. I could not decline a bride, so likely to be beloved by him.'

'You thought that?'

'I did—I have every reason to think it still.'

Meredith smiled gently, and then his face grew grave.

'Roma——' he began, and said no more.

'Make your mind easy; she never cared one atom for me.'

'Why—why? She always seemed——'

'She merely liked me as an ordinary friend—nothing more.'

'And you?'

'I cared only for Maud, who is now my promised wife. Roma and I understood one another all along. I could not explain everything; but she knew from the first that the engagement was purely nominal.'

Michael Meredith held out his hand.

'Sir, you are a man of honour, and a true gentleman. I thank you with all my heart. I could almost wish still that I might call you son.'

'Phil will be a son much more to your mind than I could ever be, Mr. Meredith,' answered Tor. 'He and Roma were made for one another. At least, I can answer for it that Roma is just the sort of wife he wants, to steady him down and give him an object in life. A little ballast is all he needs. He is the best-hearted, sunniest-tempered fellow in the world.'

'I can believe it—as his father was before him. I wonder——'

He paused; but Tor took up the word and added:

'Wonder if the second Philip Debenham will be as amenable as the first? I should not have much anxiety on that point.'

'You think——?'

'I think Roma and Signor Pagliadini spent a great deal of time wandering about in the moonlight together.'

'Did they?'

Old Meredith looked disturbed for a moment, as though he had been guilty of some indiscretion, as indeed he had.

'Really, I did not notice—I—I—. You see, Roma was engaged.'

'Only she knew she was free. She was certainly allowed to run into danger; but on the whole, I fancy, it will not turn out amiss.'

'Go and find her,' said Meredith. 'I must see her myself; go and fetch her to me. Where has Philip Debenham gone?'

'I should not be surprised to find them together,' said Tor, rising. 'If so, shall I bring both the culprits?'

'Yes, do so. It is strange, indeed, how my will always fulfils itself.'

'Indeed, yes,' answered Tor, with a slight smile.

'And you know, Mr. Torwood, I did misdoubt you somewhat from the first.'

'You certainly did, sir, in the first moment of our acquaintance. Your sagacity, you see, was not at fault.'

And then he went off on his errand.

He did not find those he sought very readily; but they were alone and together, sure enough, in a remote part of the garden. It was not difficult to see that Philip Debenham had easily usurped Signor Pagliadini's place; but even yet Roma was not quite content.

'Well,' said Tor, when his presence was first observed, 'is it all well?'

'Roma is afraid of what her father will say,' said Phil.

'He was so fond of you,' said Roma, looking up at him without any fear or shame.

'You can't have him now, Roma,' said Phil. 'He's engaged to Maud. He lost no time, I can assure you. He leaped from the brother to the lover in about ten seconds. Have you explained everything to Mr. Meredith, Tor?'

'Yes, and he is desirous of bestowing his blessing upon you. It is all right, Roma. I told you it would be all right, if you would only wait my time. He is more pleased than ever. Go to him, and see for yourself if it is not so.'

Phil and Roma returned slowly to the house to receive the paternal benediction, and Tor strolled across the park to Ladywell.

'Well, Mr. Torwood,' said a voice behind him; 'how does it feel to be no longer monarch of all you survey?'

'Is that you, Miss Marjory? This is well met. I have hardly seen you all day.'

'No, you found metal more attractive elsewhere. I am not jealous, I assure you. Well, how has the Belassis introduction passed off?'

'Oh, very well. Phil was quite as bold as I, and more cheeky than I was at my first interview. I don't think the worthy uncle will make much out of him.'

'Thanks to you, perhaps not; but he is a mere boy—not fit to have the management of a place like this.'

'He is only three months my junior.'

'He is a mere boy, for all that, and you are a man. I like men, for my part. When I was young, it wasn't the fashion to admire long-haired, knock-kneed youths with narrow chests and æsthetic tastes. I'm behind the times, I know; but I stick to my old-fashioned views. I like a man who can take a horse across country without bringing him home lame, and who knows more of nature than of art. I suppose I should be called an old Philistine nowadays.'

'I don't know, I'm sure. I don't suppose the Philistines were half bad fellows, after all. However, I think Phil will do very well at Ladywell.'

'You'd do better,' said Miss Marjory.

'You think so?'

'I know it.'

'Well, Miss Marjory, I'm very glad to be quit of it and its responsibilities, that I can tell you,' said Tor, stretching his long limbs as if to assure himself that the load was gone. 'It has been a horrid nuisance at times—all this; and if it had not been for two things accomplished, I should feel inclined to think I had taken more trouble than the matter was worth.'

'What two things are those?'

'Keeping Maud out of the hands of the Belassis party, and making your acquaintance, Miss Marjory.'

Miss Marjory bowed.

'Gaining a wife and a friend, is that it?' said she. 'You might have known me long ago if you had not been so lazy as to do all your business through an agent. Middlemen are a mistake.'

'My middle-man shall henceforward be dismissed. We will do business in future always at first hand—you and I, Miss Marjory.'

'And I shall get my own way in everything!' cried Miss Marjory, with animation. 'You don't know what you are letting yourself in for!'

'I thought I was such a competent manager?'

'You can manage property pretty well, I admit,' answered Miss Marjory; 'but I am not aware that I ever said you could manage me!'

'Perish the thought!' cried Tor, with fervour. 'Miss Marjory, did anybody ever manage you since the days of your babyhood?'

'Of a certainty nobody did so during my babyhood,' laughed Miss Marjory. 'I ruled the household before I could speak.'

'And I'm sure you did so afterwards,' said Tor, with gravity.

'Well,' said Miss Marjory, glancing up at him with quaint humour, 'I'm not sure but what I did.'

'You were born great,' he said, 'whilst I only had greatness thrust upon me, of which I am very glad to be relieved.'

'Really?'

'Really and truly. Do you doubt it?'

'No; but I know I shouldn't like to give up the reins of government when once I'd held them. I always do want my finger in everybody's pie, especially when the pie takes the form of gardens. I never go round a place but what I want to lay it out anew myself, and suggest improvements.'

'Then I shall expect you to come and lay out mine for me, Miss Marjory, whenever I settle down. Now mind, I shall consider it a bargain from this time forth.'

'You are going to settle down, then? A good thing, too. "A rolling stone," you know.'

'Well, Miss Marjory, to tell the truth, I don't think you've gathered much moss yourself, in spite of your devotion to Whitbury.'

Miss Marjory laughed, but rather liked the compliment implied.

'Yes,' said Tor, 'I am going to settle down as a steady married man, somewhere in this neighbourhood, if I can get a house, so as to be near Phil, who will of course expect me to look after him to a certain extent. Maud likes Devonshire, and so do I. But I shall require one visit a year at least from you, Miss Marjory, just to see that my garden is going on right, and that I am not gathering moss or rust or anything else that I ought not. I shall visit Whitbury, too, from time to time to see after my property there, and renew a very pleasant acquaintance with the place. And if, Miss Marjory, I should be blessed with a family, my first daughter will be called Marjory; and I have in my mind's eye one sponsor, whom I shall humbly request to stand for her. And if she should by any chance grow up unmanageable, I shall just send her off on a visit to her godmother in Whitbury, to be reduced to order and obedience by the universal manager.'

CHAPTER XII.
A MAN AND A BROTHER.

LEWIS BELASSIS did not cease his visits to Ladywell because Maud had rejected him. On the contrary, he came as often as ever, and was made decidedly more welcome than he had been before.

He was in no way put out by the arrival of the new Philip Debenham, and even heard with equanimity the news of Maud's engagement to Tor.

Phil liked this cousin of his, Belassis though he was, and Lewis liked Phil and admired him. He felt that he had more in common with him than with Tor, and so he came a good deal to Ladywell.

What he did with himself during the busy days which followed Phil's sudden arrival, nobody seemed quite to know. He was often about the place, that was certain, and frequently dropped in to lunch; but neither Phil nor Tor, Maud, Miss Marjory nor Mrs. Lorraine, saw much of him at other times, although they all declared with one voice that they thought the young man had very much improved of late. Nobody was specially interested in Lewis, so far as they knew.

Miss Marjory had not left Ladywell yet, though she had made an attempt to do so, saying that her work was done, and that she ought now to be at home. Phil and Tor, however, had combined to entreat her to stay at least another week, and she had consented, without any great amount of persuasion.

One day, as she happened to be looking out of her window over the gardens, she saw a sight which at once arrested her attention.

It was not any very uncommon sight certainly, and one which was frequently to be seen at Ladywell at that time—a young man and a young girl walking together, absorbed in earnest conversation; and yet it set Miss Marjory thinking, and as she thought, a little frown knitted her brow.

Half an hour later she heard a footfall outside her door, and called out:

'Ethel!'

'Yes, Cousin Marjory.'

'Come in—I want you.'

So Ethel came in, her blooming face somewhat more blooming than usual, and a little smile of happiness sparkling in her blue eyes.

Miss Marjory's face lost its look of gravity, and she smiled too. Sometimes Miss Marjory had been known to say of herself, that she did not feel as though she should ever be really old. In heart, she was still young.

'Where have you been, Ethel?'

'In the garden.'

'Were you alone there?'

'N—no!'—here the colour deepened somewhat, but Ethel looked up fearlessly and frankly, and added: 'Mr. Lewis Belassis was with me.'

'He has often been with you lately, has he not?'

'Ye—yes, Cousin Marjory, rather often. You see, everybody is so taken up just now! There is nobody else for him to talk to!'

Miss Marjory smiled, and then her face grew grave.

'Has he been making love to you, Ethel?'

Her face grew rosy red.

'I—I hardly know—not exactly; but I think—I can't help fancying——'

'That will do, child; you needn't tell me any more.'

Miss Marjory sat so still for a few minutes—so still, and so thoughtful—that Ethel, after looking at her once or twice, began to grow nervous.

'You are not angry, Cousin Marjory?'

'No, child, not angry; but I wish, all the same, that it hadn't happened—not just yet, at any rate,' she added, catching the look on Ethel's face.

'Cousin Marjory, we couldn't help it—indeed we couldn't! Please don't say we mustn't!'

Miss Marjory smiled, and shook her head.

'My dear child, I have no authority over you. You are of age, and your father is alive; and now that he has married again, and has made new ties, I do not imagine he will seriously oppose your choice, provided it seems at all suitable. You have your own independent fortune, even if it is not a very large one. I have no right to lay a veto on your marriage.'

'But I hope you will like it, Cousin Marjory!'

Miss Marjory laughed a little.

'To speak the truth, Ethel, I have never looked forward to having very much in common with your husband, or with Horace's wife; so you need not be disappointed on that score.'

Ethel opened her blue eyes wide. She was not quite equal to taking in the full meaning of Miss Marjory's remark.

'I thought you liked Lewis!'

'I think, considering his parentage and bringing up, he is a marvel; but I don't know anything specially remarkable about him otherwise.'

'He is very nice!' said Ethel meekly, feeling that she was making but a poor champion for the man whom she really loved fondly.

Miss Marjory sat with knitted brow, wrapped in thought of no very pleasant kind.

'Don't set your heart too much upon this man, Ethel.'

'Oh, Cousin Marjory! Why not?'

'It may be impossible for him to marry you.'

'Oh, Cousin Marjory! I thought you said you would not forbid it!'

'It will be no doing of mine, child. But, as I said before, it may be an impossibility for all that. Now don't begin to cry. I have not said that it cannot go on, only that it may not be able to do so. Lewis would be the first to tell you so himself, if he knew what I know.'

'What is that?'

'Never mind; it does not concern you. Be a brave woman, Ethel, and not a child! So you are quite sure that this Lewis wants to marry you?'

'I am almost sure.'

'Has he asked you?'

'Not quite.'

'But almost?'

'Yes.'

'And you have almost answered him?'

'Yes.'

'That sort of thing wouldn't suit me,' said Miss Marjory. 'When I was young, we didn't do things by halves as you do now. When I was your age, men asked the plain question, and got a straight answer—very straight it generally was, if I remember right! However, times change, and so do people and their ways. Well, well! if you don't mind shilly-shallying, I don't see why I need. Has he got anything to marry on—this Lewis of yours?'

'Not very much without Maud's money, and he isn't going to touch that. He is very high-principled, Cousin Marjory. He is going to give that all back, as soon as it is made over to him.'

'Well, that is honourable enough. I like him for that. He has not a ghost of a right to that money, though it is legally his. Well, and when he makes over that, what has he left?'

'Only about a hundred a year—something an uncle left him once. I have three hundred a year, you know, Cousin Marjory; and I have not spent nearly that whilst I have been living with you. Lewis doesn't think his father will do anything for him, after he has given over Maud's money, he will be so angry; but he means to try and get something to do. I thought—we thought—you know you said——'

'Said I would help him to something?

Well, I'll do what I can, if he shows himself worthy. I'll do that in any case, whether you marry him or not, for he'll need a helping hand. I can't say I like the idea of your marrying a Belassis; but, as I said before, that's not my business, and no good ever comes of trying to shape out other people's lives for them. But mind what I say, don't be led on past recall, and don't pledge yourself, or set your heart on it yet. It may be impossible.'

'Oh, I hope not!'

'I hope not too.'

'Can't you tell me more, Cousin Marjory?'

'No, not now, child; but I hope to be able to do so shortly.'

Lewis Belassis was wandering aimlessly along a field-path, not very far from Ladywell, and indulging in a dream of a brighter future than had ever before seemed to await him, when he was accosted by a respectable-looking man, who had the air and appearance of a well-to-do tradesman.

'If you please, sir, can you direct me to Ladywell Manor?' said the man.

Lewis eyed him curiously, for there was an odd resemblance to his father in the man's voice and appearance, which suggested to his mind the fanciful idea that he might be a poor relation, who had been studiously kept in the background all this while, and whose very existence was unknown to him.

It would be just like his father to be ashamed of a poor kinsman, Lewis thought; but the resemblance was not strong enough to afford any real reason for the fancy thus conjured up.

'Ladywell Manor—yes, certainly, you can get to it this way; but the field-paths are rather intricate, and you would most likely stray. If you'll walk to the end of the field with me, I can put you into a much more direct way of finding it.'

'Thank you, sir,' said the man, and turned back readily.

'I've just come from Ladywell,' remarked Lewis, inwardly wondering what could be the man's business there. 'It's a fine old place.'

'Yes, sir? I'm a stranger in these parts. I come from Whitbury; it is Miss Marjory Descartes that I've come to see. She's our great lady at Whitbury.'

'Ah,' said Lewis, his first faint impression dying away; 'she's a great lady, I fancy, wherever she goes.'

'Like enough, sir,' answered the other; and they walked on in silence.

As they reached the road, two friends of Lewis's rode by.

'How do, Belassis?' said one.

'Morning, Belassis,' said the other.

Then the strange man turned and looked at him.

'Is your name Belassis, sir?'

'Yes, certainly.'

Lewis's first suspicion woke again into new life.

'So is mine,' said the man—'Alfred Belassis.'

'Why, I thought there was something of a Belassis look about you,' said Lewis heartily, for he was not a cad, and was above coldshouldering a poor relation. 'Shake hands; I fancy we are some sort of cousins. I'll walk your way, and we'll find out.'

'Well, sir,' said the man slowly, 'if you're the son of Mr. Alfred Belassis of these parts, maybe I'd best walk your way, and see him.'

'You are a relation of ours, then?'

'Yes, sir; and I'm afraid, perhaps, a nearer one than you'll quite relish.'

Lewis laughed good-naturedly.

'Never mind my father—he always was a growler, as I dare say you know; but so far as I am concerned, you will be very welcome.'

'Thank you, sir; you mean kindly, I see, only you don't know yet who I am.'

'No, I don't; but I wish you'd tell me.'

'Well, sir, I'm your half-brother—if you want to know.'

'My—half—brother!'

'Yes, sir. I'm afraid you won't like it; but I've not come here to force myself upon you, or make myself unpleasant. I've got a word to say to my father, whom I never knew; and when I've said it, I'll go. He'll be glad of my message, even if he isn't glad to see his own son.'

'My half-brother!' repeated Lewis once more, with even greater astonishment.

'Yes, sir; Mr. Alfred Belassis married my mother before he married yours.'

'I never knew he had a first wife! I don't believe anyone knew.'

'Like enough, sir. He behaved real bad, he did—deserted my mother less than three months after he married her, and never sent her word or line, or took the least bit of notice of her. She thought he had died, and sort of believed in him all along, I've heard tell. But Miss Marjory had me brought up—my poor mother was always weakly; and she told me the whole story when I grew up. We've got a bad father, you and I have, sir.'

'My name is Lewis. If we are brothers, you should not call me "sir,"' said Lewis, feeling, as he had often felt of late, that his father was a despicable character.

'I know my place, sir,' answered the man, not without dignity. 'I like you for not flying out, because we've got the same father; but we've been brought up different. You're a gentleman, whilst I keep a shop. I've made a tidy lot of money in business; but I know my place, and I know I'm not like you.'

'You may thank your stars you're not,' said poor Lewis. 'It seems to me I've nothing to call my own, but the name my father has disgraced.'

'We needn't disgrace it, sir,' said the man respectfully. 'I never was ashamed of it—downright ashamed—till I got a letter from Miss Marjory a week ago.'

'And what did that tell you?'

'Why, that your father, sir—and mine—didn't ever trouble to find out that my poor mother was dead, before he married yours. He does not even know now that she is his lawful wife.'

Lewis flushed hotly.

'But she is?'

'Yes, sir, she is: I'd not have liked to come here and face you all, if things had turned out different; but it is all right in that sense, though he don't really know it. Miss Marjory, she wrote and told me about things here, and bid me try to find out the exact date of my mother's death, from the people who brought me up. She thought they'd be most likely to know. They didn't know exactly, but I got to know the place where she died, and I went down to see the registers and find out. She died on the 2nd of May, 1850, and Mr. Belassis married again about a fortnight later. But he didn't know anything about this death.'

Lewis walked on in silence. He felt very much inclined not to go home at all, after what he had just heard, so profoundly disgusted was he with his father; but on the whole he decided that he would do so, and take this elder brother with him.

It was luncheon-time when he arrived, and they were a little late, so that the servant had withdrawn.

Lewis entered boldly, with the young tradesman close behind him.

'Allow me,' said he to his father, 'to introduce to you your first-born son, Alfred Belassis.'

Matilda and Bertha screamed, Mrs. Belassis turned pale, her husband purple.

'D—— your impudence!' he cried, starting up. 'What do you mean by coming here with such a story? I'll kick you out of my house if you dare ever enter it again!'

It seemed uncertain to which of the two sons the threat was made. The elder one took it as addressed to him.

'I've no particular wish ever to come again, sir. I am not proud of the relationship, and I don't care to claim it. I only came now to bring you something which I think you may like to possess;' and he took from his pocket-book and handed to Mr. Belassis a certified copy of the register of the death of his first wife.

He took it, looked at it, and handed it across to his wife. An immense load seemed lifted at once from his shoulders; but instead of feeling any gratitude towards the man who had brought the good news, or any spark of affection for the son of whose very existence he had not been aware till now, he was only filled with a burning rage against anyone who had dared to bring home to him, and in a manner to make public, the most disgraceful episode of his early life.

He was too angry even to consider his own interests, or to try and conciliate the man who possessed knowledge so much to his discredit. He turned furiously upon Alfred Belassis, and swore at him more loudly than before.

'Get out of my house, you blackguard! coming forcing your way in under false pretences, and making up scandalous stories to extort money! I know the ways of gentlemen like you; and if you don't make the best of your way out double-quick, I'll have you kicked out by the servants!'

But Lewis laid his hand upon his half-brother's arm to detain him.

'This man is your son as much as I am!' said he boldly. 'He is my brother, and I won't stand by and hear him insulted! If you turn him out of your house, I shall go too!'

Mrs. Belassis smiled contemptuously. She thought her son was only making himself ridiculous, and she considered the presence of that other man in the room a positive insult to herself.

'You can go to the devil, both of you!' growled Belassis fiercely. 'What do I care?'

Lewis took Alfred's arm, and led him from the room and from the house.

Mrs. Belassis smiled even more contemptuously.

'He will come back to-morrow like a whipped puppy, with his tail between his legs.'

'What does it all mean?' asked Bertha. 'Why do you and papa always quarrel with everybody? Who is that man?'

'A distant relative of your father's, who is very troublesome and pushing. We have helped him till we are tired, and now, I think, he will come no more,' answered Mrs. Belassis grandly.

'Why did Lewis say——'

'Lewis is a fool!' snapped Mr. Belassis; and then he added, a little uneasily: 'but I don't want to quarrel with him, for all that.'

He looked at his wife, who merely smiled, and said:

'You need not be afraid of Lewis. I can turn him round my little finger!'

The relief given by this certificate was intense, to the proud, hard woman who had ruled at Thornton House with a rod of iron. Her contempt for the husband she had married was unbounded; but, at least, she was his lawful wife, and therefore policy bound her over to his cause. She knew quite well why Lewis must be kept in a good humour; for his father's good name was at his mercy, or would be very shortly, when the handing-over of Maud's trust-money could no longer be delayed.

Mrs. Belassis, however, had small opinion of Lewis's force of character, and attached no importance to this foolish quarrel.

As the newly-acquainted brothers walked across the park towards Ladywell, Alfred said:

'You shouldn't have quarrelled with them for my sake, sir.'

'I wasn't going to stand seeing you treated like that! You're as much his son as I am!'

'Yes, sir, true enough; but, of course, things have changed; and he doesn't like to be made to think of the past.'

'He needn't have insulted you.'

'No, sir, he needn't; but when a man's temper is up, he doesn't pick his words. We'd better have had it out more quiet-like, without the missis and the young ladies sitting by.'

'Well, one can't think of everything, and truth's truth. I know I should have quarrelled with him sooner or later; it doesn't much matter how it happened.'

'But you'll make it up again, surely, sir?'

'I wish you wouldn't call me "sir." I don't know if I shall make it up. We've got a quarrel brewing on our own account. There's a lot of money come to me by law, which isn't mine by right—only by a piece of trickery. I'm not going to keep it. I'm going to give it back to the rightful owner, and my father will be furious—I know he will.'

'And when you've given up the money, and quarrelled with your father, how are you going to live, if I may be so bold as to ask?'

'I must earn my living somehow—sweep a crossing if need be. Well, no, I've got just enough to keep me above that; and I hope to get a decent berth of some kind, if such a thing's to be had. I did want to get married'—here Lewis sighed—'but, of course, that must wait till I've something to marry upon—eh, Alfred?'

He found it easier to talk to this friendly tradesman-relative of his affairs, than he would have done had he been of equal social standing. There was a straightforward honesty about the man which pleased him.

Alfred seemed to ponder for a while.

'You see, sir, it wants capital in these days to get a good berth—unless one's a lad, and can work up from the bottom. Right must be done, but you'd have found the money very useful.'

'I know that well enough,' sighed Lewis; 'but I can't rob my own cousin of what would have been hers, but for my father's scheming. They all say it was that, and I believe it.'

'No, sir; I see you couldn't. I don't believe riches got like that ever prosper. Well, we'll see what can be done. You've stood by me like a brother, and it would be a poor return if I couldn't do the same by you.'

'Thanks, Alfred,' said Lewis; but he smiled inwardly, wondering how this shopkeeper brother's support could be of any assistance to him.

CHAPTER XIII.
LEWIS'S FATE.

THE arrival of Lewis with Alfred Belassis at Ladywell that day, caused a considerable amount of speculation and astonishment.

When, in addition, Lewis announced the fact that he had quarrelled with his father, and meant to return no more to Thornton House, quite a sensation was produced; and Miss Marjory did not hesitate to tell him that she considered he had judged wisely and well.

'You shall stay here, old fellow,' said Phil warmly, 'till we can find you a berth of some kind; and don't you be in any hurry. Give yourself plenty of time to look round; something good will be sure to turn up if you do. You've behaved like a brick about that money, and the least we can do is to make you some return.'

'The money wasn't mine, as you all know,' said Lewis. 'I hope I know better than to profit by a low trick like that, even though my father was the one who practised it.'

'I think we ought to divide it,' said Maud, 'just in case papa did mean some of it for you.'

Miss Marjory had beckoned Alfred Belassis to her side. Mrs. Lorraine was standing near, looking anxious. She knew on what errand he had come.

'Have you found out about your mother's death?' she asked in a low voice.

'Yes; it was on the 2nd of May, 1850.'

Mrs. Lorraine drew a long breath of relief.

'Well,' said Miss Marjory, 'I'm glad to hear it, for the sake of the innocent, who would suffer more than the guilty; but he drove it close enough. What a miserable coward he is!'

Alfred Belassis stood silent, looking and feeling rather awkward, in the midst of such a company.

'I should like to speak a word to you in private, ma'am,' he said, 'if it isn't troubling you too much. I ought to be getting back to Whitbury as fast as I can, now that I've done what you asked.'

'Come into this room, then,' said Miss Marjory, opening a door which stood near. 'Let me hear what it is you have to say.'

Belassis followed her in, and sat down at her bidding. He was a thick-set, clever-looking man, with more honesty than beauty to recommend him.

'Well, Belassis,' said Miss Marjory, 'what is it?'

'If you please, ma'am, I want to know if I couldn't be of some use to that young gentleman there, who is a sort of brother to me, after all.'

'Lewis, you mean? Well, I don't know exactly how you could serve him. I'm afraid he would be little good to you as a partner.'

Alfred Belassis looked almost shocked.

'Oh no, ma'am; of course I couldn't think of such a thing. A young gentleman like him could never take to trade; it wouldn't be right nor proper. I know better than that; but he's had education, you know, and advantages of other kinds, and I'm thinking something might be found for him more suitable.'

Miss Marjory reflected. She, too, could not be indifferent now to the future of Lewis Belassis.

'They tell me he has good abilities. He might perhaps get on in some line, if he had a fair start. I don't mind doing my best for him; but in what way did you mean to help, Belassis?'

'With money, ma'am. A deal more can be done for a man who's got a few thousands at his back, than one who has only got his brains to look to. I should like to see to the money part of it—because, you know, he's my brother after a fashion.'

'This is very generous of you, Belassis; but are you a man of means?'

'Thanks to you, ma'am, I've done very well. You got me the place of assistant to Mr. Hanly when I was but eighteen, and I succeeded to the business when I was five-and-twenty. You stood my friend, and I never wanted for work; and things have been growing and growing, until I've almost more to do than I know how to get through sometimes. I'm a plain man myself, and I've never married; and the money has all gone into the bank, and been invested from time to time. There's three thousand as I can lay my hands upon any day, and not leave myself pinched. I'd as soon Mr. Lewis had it to help him to a start, as spend it any other way. So if any good thing turns up as wants a little capital launched, you know where the money's to come from. I think that's all, ma'am. I won't detain you longer. I could best speak out to you, because I don't feel so strange like with you, as I do with the other folks in there.'

'Stop—stop, Belassis! not quite so fast!' cried Miss Marjory. 'This is very generous of you, but really I'm not sure if you should do it. Suppose he is very long in repaying you.'

'I was not thinking about repayment,' said Belassis. 'I'd risk the chance of that.'

'But really, Belassis, you must be practical, and consider what you are doing. Three thousand is a large sum, and Lewis has no claim upon you.'

'Well, ma'am, he wasn't ashamed to own me as his brother, nor to stand by me like a brother when the old man swore at us. It isn't every young gentleman as would have cared to accept a man like me as a relation, on my bare word; and it ain't many as would have stood up for me as he did.'

'He behaved well towards you, I admit; but still——'

'I ought to do well by him, then. I never knew before as I'd got a brother, and it'll be a real pleasure if I can help him. I'm a plain man, and I don't love money for its own sake. I'd much rather it was helping Mr. Lewis, than lying by idle at the bank. Will you let him know about it, if ever he wants it to make his start?'

'Well, if you're bent on it, Belassis, I'll say no more. But won't you tell Lewis yourself?'

'I'd sooner you did it, ma'am. It's rather early days for me to speak, and we don't know yet what he'll want, or even if he wants anything. He may make it up with his father, and not want any help. I'd sooner leave it in your hands, if you please. Mind you let him know that it doesn't matter at all about paying it back. I don't want him hampered by debt. I'd sooner give it outright.'

'Oh, Belassis, Belassis! And you call yourself a man of business!'

'Yes, ma'am, and so I am; but this isn't business at all, and I don't want it to be. The poor young gentleman is worse off, to my thinking, than if he'd got no father; and I'm his elder brother, and he's accepted me as one, only thinking me a poor shopkeeper. I should like to play an elder brother's part, and it isn't a matter of business at all.'

He got up as he said the last words, and Miss Marjory followed his example.

'Well, you talk like an honest and kind-hearted man, Belassis, and your brother ought to be proud of the relationship.'

'Good-day, then, ma'am. I must be getting back to Whitbury now. You'll kindly see after things for me here, I know.'

So Alfred Belassis escaped from Ladywell, Lewis walking with him part of the way to the station.

'I should like to come and see you, Alfred, one of these days,' said Lewis. 'You're the only relation I am likely to see much of for some time to come. Have you any objection to a visit?'

'I shall be honoured by your presence, sir.'

'I'm afraid it won't confer much honour; but I should like to see Whitbury, and call upon Miss Marjory, and—and—I mean, see her in her own house.'

'Yes, sir.'

And so they parted, the elder man taking his way towards the inn and the coach-road, and Lewis standing at the corner, looking doubtful and irresolute.

'Perhaps I'd better go back and have it out at once. It must be said sooner or later, and I have my traps to collect. I don't see any use in putting off the evil day; it must come sometime. I'll go straight up and have done with it.'

And he turned his steps towards Thornton House.

He did not seek his father at once upon his arrival, but went straight up to his own room. All his possessions there were his own property, for his uncle's legacy had supplied him with funds for his personal wants ever since he was of age, and therefore he had the entire right to claim as his own all that was there.

He packed up in his portmanteaux everything that he valued or that could be of any use in the future, and then he rang and ordered the man to carry down the boxes by the back staircase, and get them conveyed to Ladywell.

This packing-up had occupied more than two hours, and Mr. and Mrs. Belassis, who had seen from the window their son's arrival, smiled a little to themselves at his speedy return, and at the quiet way in which it had been effected.

'I told you he would come back like a whipped puppy,' said Mrs. Belassis. 'I do not think we shall have any further trouble with Lewis.'

'I'm sure I hope not,' sighed the husband. 'I've had enough trouble these past months to carry a man into his grave. But I do think when we've searched Ladywell and found that will, we really shall have no more to fear. You're sure Betsy Long is to be trusted to let us in and to hold her tongue?'

'Oh yes! I make it well worth her while. She loves money far too well to betray us. We can spend as many nights as we like in the library, and nobody be any the wiser.'

'Ah!' and Belassis drew a long breath, 'it really seems as if things were coming right at last!'

And then the door opened, and Lewis came in.

'Well, sir!' said the father grandly.

Mrs. Belassis folded her hands with a smile, and added, interrogatively:

'Well, Lewis?'

'Well, sir, I've come to say a rather less hasty good-bye; and to tell you of a resolution I have taken.'

Both countenances changed slightly.

'Say good-bye!' echoed Belassis, with the ghost of a laugh. 'What do you mean?'

'Don't be a fool, Lewis,' advised his mother concisely.

'I'm going to stay at Ladywell until I can find something to do, for I'm sick of the life here, and don't mean to stay to be ordered out of the house a second time. People there are very kind, and I shall be sure to find some sort of a berth before very long. Now I want to know when that ten thousand pounds, with interest and compound interest for eighteen years, will be paid in to me?'

Mr. Belassis sat silent; his jaw had fallen somewhat, his eyes were full of anxiety. His wife spoke in his place:

'Why do you ask?'

'I should have thought it was a very natural question. As Maud is to be married to some one else very shortly, I should think the money might be paid up at once.'

'It will be paid when your father thinks right.'

'That won't quite do for me,' said Lewis boldly; 'the money is mine, and I want it. I want to get the transfer made out, and the thing off my mind, before I make my own start. Now, sir, will you kindly tell me what you mean to do?'

'The transfer!' gasped Belassis; 'what the devil do you mean?'

'I thought I had made myself plain the other night,' said Lewis. 'The money is Maud's, not mine, and I shall simply transfer it to her.'

'You will do no such thing, Lewis,' said Mrs. Belassis, with significance.

'I shall do it!' said Lewis firmly. 'Everybody knows it, and I shall stand by my word.'

'You will have no power to do so,' answered the mother. 'You had better have held your tongue about it, as I advised you.'

'What do you mean?'

'I mean that there is no money to receive. Your clever and honest father has speculated with it—and lost it. That is all.'

Lewis stood still in astonishment and dismay.

'But I can claim it—he is bound to repay it!'

'If you choose you can, of course; but you will not. Maud's five thousand must be paid, and will be, though it is a serious loss to us; but you will never see a penny of yours.'

'It is not mine, it is Maud's. I shall claim it for her. She shall not be fleeced like this!'

'Claim it, then, and bring ruin and disgrace upon your father! It will be a noble part from a son!'

'Has not my father brought disgrace upon himself without anyone's help? Has he not nearly brought upon you, and upon me, the worst disgrace which the world holds? It is no doing of his that I am not at present a nameless outcast—it is merely a chance for which we have to thank fortune, and not him. And he appeals to me to save him from disgrace! I will not listen! I will have justice! It is he who has disgraced himself, not I!'

'Lewis, consider!' began Mrs. Belassis, who, though she cared little for her husband, and heartily despised him, had no wish to see him disgraced and impoverished in order to swell the wealth of Maud and Torwood.

'I will consider nothing but justice! I will have what is legally mine, in order to give it to her whose right it is. My father deserves no mercy at my hands, and he shall not get it!'

'This, then, is my reward for scheming and sinning for your future happiness!' burst out Belassis, in an agony of rage and fear.

'More shame for you to have so schemed and sinned,' answered Lewis; but his indignation had cooled somewhat, and it was easy to see that he took no pleasure in the thought of bringing ruin and disgrace upon his own house.

'Lewis,' said Mrs. Belassis coldly and calmly, 'you have spoken the truth—your father deserves no mercy at your hands. He had, for aught he knew at the time, committed the vilest action a man could perpetrate. He is disgraced, as you say, already, and the story of crime will be all over the place to-morrow. Ruin and disgrace he heartily merits; but what about me?'

'You, mother?'

'Yes; I am your mother. I shall be involved in whatever ruin and disgrace overtakes your father—I and your sisters both. You must think of that, before you take any irrevocable step.'

Lewis stood silent.

'I have had a good deal to bear already as the fruit of your father's misconduct; but we have contrived to weather matters pretty well up till now. If you strike this threatened blow, however, all is lost, and you will be the ruin of your whole family.'

Still Lewis said nothing.

'Well,' she asked, after a pause, 'what have you to say now?'

'Nothing.'

'Nothing?'

'No; I must think.'

'Yes, you had better think,' said Mrs. Belassis, knowing well that reflection was likely to be favourable to her own cause.

'Good-bye,' he said suddenly. 'I shall be at Ladywell for some time to come, I expect.'

And then he turned and quitted the room, without another word.

'He is safe,' said Mrs. Belassis; 'he will not do it now. We are safe, so far as he is concerned.'

Lewis went back to Ladywell, and told his story in confidence to Miss Marjory. People had a way of going to Miss Marjory when they were in doubt or perplexity, because such feelings seemed unknown to her.

She listened intently, and then abused Belassis with all the force of her emphatic vocabulary.

'What must I do?' asked Lewis. 'Must I denounce and ruin him?'

'He deserves it,' answered Miss Marjory hotly. 'He deserves it richly; but a man's mother, Lewis, is his mother, and his first duty is to protect her.'

And to the son Miss Marjory breathed none of the suspicions she had formed as to the mother's integrity. As she afterwards told Tor, she was old-fashioned enough to think that loyalty to a mother stood before every other claim.

'Well, yes, I suppose it does,' said Lewis gravely. 'I can't help feeling it myself. I've not been so fond of her as I ought, perhaps; but she's my mother still, and it doesn't seem fair that she should suffer so much for what my father has done. But I should have liked Maud to have her own.'

'So should I. It would be a nice little fortune for her; but I don't see your way quite clear, though your father deserves no mercy. However, I'm glad to know that you did really mean to make restitution of what you felt did not rightly belong to you. It is much to your credit.—And so you have been making love to my young cousin, I understand, under my very nose?'

Poor Lewis flushed scarlet at this sudden and totally unexpected thrust.

'I—I— Was it very wrong? I couldn't help feeling——'

'Oh, keep your feelings for Ethel. I'm not at all interested in them. What I want to know is, what your future prospects are?'

'Bad, I'm afraid,' said Lewis candidly; 'much worse than when I began to speak to your cousin; for I've quarrelled with my father, and he has been playing fast and loose with his money, I suspect. But I might get something in time, if Ethel could wait. She said she would——'

'Oh yes, I dare say she will. She's a faithful little puss, and very steady and affectionate. But you must look about you seriously. Have you any plans?'

Lewis shook his head; and then Miss Marjory, after putting him through an examination on his acquirements, which he got through fairly well, informed him that she would write to an old friend of hers in London, who had a publishing business of a lucrative kind, and had been meditating taking in a young partner. He was childless, and a widower to boot, and such a berth was likely to be a good one. Miss Marjory and he were old friends, and he had known Ethel's father and mother.

Lewis was delighted. Such an opening was just what he wanted, and from what he could learn from Miss Marjory, the duties were of a kind which he would be able to master without great difficulty, and would be congenial to him. His spirits rose greatly, and he overwhelmed Miss Marjory with thanks; and by her permission went in search of Ethel.

The answer to Miss Marjory's letter was eagerly awaited. It came promptly, and was favourable to Miss Marjory's young friend, who was invited to go to London for a personal interview. Of course it was expected that he would have a few thousands to put into the business, in return for a junior partnership and its prospects.

Lewis's face fell when he read this final clause.

With a great sigh he handed back the letter.

'Thank you very much, Miss Marjory; but of course that puts it out of the question.'

'Not at all. You have three thousand to back you. I dare say that will be enough.'

'You are joking, Miss Marjory. What little I have of my own is only mine in trust. I cannot sink the principal; and then it would not come to three thousand.'

'I was not thinking of your own money.'

'What then?'

'Of what your brother—half-brother, I should say—wishes to advance for you, to give you a start in life. He left it for me to tell you, if it should be necessary. Alfred Belassis is anxious to give or lend you that amount of money. You must settle between yourselves which it is to be.'

'Alfred Belassis!' cried Lewis, astonished. 'Why, he is only a shopkeeper!'

'Some shopkeepers make large fortunes. Trade is more lucrative than the gentlemanly professions.'

'I had no idea he had money.'

'I know, and so did he; and he thought all the better of you because you did not know. After all, Lewis, there is some good in you, and it seems to me that you are on the highroad to success.'

'But ought I to take it?'

'Oh, settle all that with Alfred. You had better go and see him, before going to London. I would start to-day if I were you. Time is valuable, you know.'

Lewis received very warm congratulations from all at Ladywell, on his sudden good fortune; and Maud was particularly delighted, only second to Ethel in her satisfaction.

'It is all Miss Marjory's doing,' she cried. 'It seems to me everything is Miss Marjory's doing. Tor always did say you could do anything you had a mind to, and I believe you can. I know you told me my fortune wonderfully well.'

So great satisfaction reigned at Ladywell, and Lewis, in high spirits, set out on his journey.

The result was satisfactory, and a good position in the publishing firm was given to him, and his engagement to Ethel Hardcastle formally announced.

Lewis, for the first time in his life, found himself a busy and a happy man.

CHAPTER XIV.
THE LOST WILL.

PHIL and Tor had sat up late one night, as was often the case, and it was not until nearly one o'clock that they retired to their respective rooms.

When Tor reached his, he found that a fall of soot had taken place, which had blackened things so much, and left so unpleasant an odour in the room, that to remain there was impossible.

It was too late to disturb the servants, or to have another room made ready for him; but Tor was too much the traveller to care where or how he slept. He merely made his way to an empty bedroom, kicked off his boots, and lay down upon the bed in the smoking-coat he had previously donned.

In five minutes he was sound asleep, with the facility of one used to 'roughing it;' but with the instinct of a man not unused to danger, he suddenly woke up, with all his faculties about him, and presently became aware of curious sounds in the room beneath him.

A moment's thought convinced him that these sounds, whatever they were, came from the library, which was directly underneath the room he accidentally occupied, and which lay in a wing of the building not much used.

There were certainly sounds proceeding from the room below; the longer Tor listened the more was he convinced of this—stealthy sounds, which he could not exactly understand, yet which were, from time to time, distinctly audible.

After a few minutes spent in listening, Tor rose, and without resuming his boots, passed quietly from the room. A dying moon gave a feeble light to corridor and staircase; and after a visit to his own room to fetch his revolver, the young man walked silently down to the library.

The door stood slightly ajar, as if the occupants, whoever they might be, were anxious to hear if any sound should arise in the house. Tor, however, took care to make no noise, and he did not hesitate to push open the door and slip silently into the room, for the feeble light the midnight guests had brought with them was far away at the upper end, and the door and all in its neighbourhood lay wrapped in the deepest gloom.

Once inside, Tor looked well at the intruders, and recognised, with an odd mixture of feeling, Mr. and Mrs. Belassis.

'What in the name of all the powers brings *them* here?' he thought, but he stood motionless, half through surprise, half from an instinct of caution, which warned him that it would be wise to find out, if possible, the reason for this strange nocturnal visit.

Both husband and wife were closely examining a heavy volume they had lifted from the shelf. They shook it, examined its cover, and otherwise pulled it about; after which it was restored to its place, and the next volume lifted down, to be submitted to a similar process.

Tor watched them with a deepening interest. They seemed so absorbed by their task, that many minutes passed before either of them spoke. As, however, Belassis replaced upon a shelf the last of the volumes it contained, he sighed heavily, and remarked:

'I don't believe we shall ever find it.'

'Well, if we don't, nobody else will, and that's all I care about; but until we have examined every book the library contains, we can never feel safe.'

Belassis sighed again.

'It will be an endless task!'

'No, only a long one; and we can come here as often, in reason, as we please; and Betsy Long can look at the books as she dusts them, if we can't get here safely ourselves.'

Tor's gaze deepened in intensity. Metaphorically speaking, he pricked up his ears at this.

'I believe we shall come to grief, somehow. That girl will betray us.'

'Not she; she knows better than to forfeit double wages, and lose both her places.'

But Belassis was not to be comforted.

'I don't believe we shall ever do any good by this; and I'm getting quite done up with these disturbed nights.'

Mrs. Belassis looked him all over with a cold contempt, which seemed to wither him up. When she spoke, it was with a crushing disdain.

'Really, Mr. Belassis, I have half a mind to take you at your word, and give up this attempt—and leave others to find Philip Debenham's last will. It seems to me that you would rather live, with total ruin hanging over your head, than give up a few nights' rest and take a little trouble. Anyone more hopelessly pusillanimous, it has never been my lot to come across!'

'It seems such a hopeless search, my dear,' began Belassis feebly. 'If we really *knew* the will was here, it would be different.'

'We do know it!' snapped Mrs. Belassis. 'Philip Debenham told old Tom Maynard that he had hidden it here. We have that in his own handwriting. What more do you want?'

'Old Maynard could never find the will, though.'

'Old Maynard had not the same motive that we have. He would soon grow tired of the search.'

'He thought Debenham must have destroyed it.'

'He did not know what we do.'

'What do you mean?'

'He did not know how Philip Debenham feared, and hated, and distrusted us, during the last years of his life.'

There was a pause, which Mrs. Belassis broke.

'Come, Alfred, do have a little common-sense. You know, as well as I do, that Philip Debenham simply made that will at your dictation, because he was weak and foolish, and believed you had much more power to do him mischief than you really had, if he had only played the man and taken his affairs into his own hands. We both knew he would not allow that will to stand, if he could possibly make another, and we always expected that a later one would turn up amongst his papers, and were prepared to act accordingly; but it did not. Nobody brought one forward, and we never found any evidence of the existence of a second will. You know, however, that we have never felt absolutely at ease on the subject, although, as years passed by, it seemed most improbable that anything could or would turn up. Then, when I found that letter of old Maynard's to young Philip, and discovered the pencil memorandum inside, which he had never read, it became evident that our suspicions had all along been correct. He had made a new will, and had hidden it, with more cunning than I should have given him credit for, at Ladywell, out of our reach. Knowing all this, how can you pretend that it is not worth searching for?'

'He might have removed it himself,' suggested Belassis humbly.

'You know better than that. If he had once found a safe place of hiding, out of your reach, he would never have been tempted to remove it. Hating you more and more as he did at the close of his life, is it likely he would ever have changed his mind about the will?'

And then the search continued in silence for a long while, whilst Tor stood concealed in his recess, watching them with lynx-like eyes.

He did not choose to leave the room, even for a moment, lest in that moment the missing paper should be found. He did not feel inclined, now that he was no longer master of the house, to step out and confront them, and demand the reason of this strange nocturnal visit.

So he waited and watched in silence, for what seemed a long time, until a faint blue film stealing into the room, announced the approach of dawn.

'We must be going now,' said Mrs. Belassis. 'We have done a good two hours' work, and have made a considerable way with the task. Four or five more nights ought to see the end of it. We have done nearly half in the four nights we have spent here already. I wish the light did not come so soon. It is hardly safe to be abroad after dawn. Come, Alfred, we must be going.'

Tor slipped away from the room as they replaced the last volume on the shelf, and mounted a few steps of the staircase. Two minutes later Mr. and Mrs. Belassis came out, and locked the door carefully behind them. Then they took their way towards the offices, and Tor followed quietly, at a discreet distance.

Betsy Long emerged from one of the rooms at the sound of their footsteps, yawning portentously.

Mrs. Belassis slipped something into her hand as she passed, and the girl curtseyed and said:

'Thank you, ma'am.'

Then the worthy couple made their exit by the back-door, which Betsy carefully locked behind them. Turning round, she uttered a loud scream, for her ex-master stood before her.

'Nice goings on, these, Betsy,' remarked Tor quietly. 'What have you got to say for yourself, eh?'

Betsy trembled and whimpered, and did not seem to have anything at all to say.

'Now, stop all that noise,' said Tor, with that quiet authority in his tone which always ensured instant obedience, 'and answer me truthfully, if you can. Are you and Mrs. Belassis in league together?'

'Yes, sir, if you please, sir,' answered Betsy faintly.

'And you have been her tool and spy ever since you came here?'

'Yes, sir.'

'What have you done for her so far, since you came, besides letting her in these four times to search the library?'

Betsy trembled still more, but felt compelled to answer.

'Please, sir, not much. I read a few letters, and listened, when I could, to what went on. My missis—I mean Mrs. Belassis—said as she thought all wasn't right, and bid me watch and find out all I could; but it didn't seem to me there was much to do except to look for the paper—what's hidden away in the library.'

'Well, you're a nice honest young woman, anyhow!' remarked Tor, seeing that the girl had not anything of much importance either to tell or to conceal. 'Now, you go straight up to your room, and stay there till you have leave to quit it. And pack up your things ready to go back to your old mistress when the right time comes; but if you dare to disobey and leave before you have permission, it will be the worse for you.'

And with that Tor strode back to his room, and finished his night in peace.

In the morning, at the breakfast-table, he told his story, which was listened to with great excitement and interest.

'You never let them go scot-free!' cried Miss Marjory. 'Oh, Mr. Torwood, I thought better things of you! Why did you not confront them at their task?'

'Because I thought that, on the whole, it would be better to confront them later on with the will in my hand, and the information on my lips, that it was to their nocturnal visits I owed the clue which had enabled us to find it. I thought that, on the whole, that would be the most crushing way of doing it.'

'Perhaps!' said Miss Marjory, still half-reluctantly; 'but I never could have resisted the temptation, if I had been there.'

'And now the will will be found!' cried Phil, 'and Maud will have her rights again. Oh, if this isn't just first-rate! Tor, you rascal, why didn't you summon me to confront my virtuous aunt and uncle?'

'I felt it was not safe to let them out of my sight; and I'm not sure, in any case, if I could have trusted your discretion.'

'You see, he's boss still, for all his protestations,' said Phil to Miss Marjory. 'I always have to play second fiddle to him, in reality.'

'And a good thing too,' answered Miss Marjory, with emphasis.

Mrs. Lorraine had listened with intense interest to Tor's account of what he had overheard the Belassis' say to one another. When she really understood that the will—whose existence had always been suspected—was supposed to be hidden away in the library at Ladywell, a little pink flush rose in her cheeks, and she hastily left the room, returning, however, in a few minutes with an old-fashioned manuscript-book.

'My dear,' she began, half-timidly, half-eagerly, 'I think I have something here which may prove a clue. I have not thought of it for many years; but perhaps there was a meaning in it which I did not understand. I will read you a little bit out of my diary, about the death of your dear father, Philip. I think I can understand better now what it was he meant.'

Everyone listened with interest to the extract, which Mrs. Lorraine proceeded to read:

"'My dear brother-in-law died this morning, at nine o'clock. I was with him alone during his last hours, for it was no place for young children, and he could not endure Alfred Belassis near him, and became so painfully excited if he even appeared, that we had to forbid him the house.

"'His mind, which had seemed much clouded since the stroke, cleared somewhat, I fancied, during the last hours of his life. He could not speak, although he made great efforts to do so; and he could not write, for his hand was paralyzed. I hope I did not do wrong in deceiving him; but he was so greatly distressed, almost whilst he was dying, that I had to pretend I had understood him.

"'He struggled time after time to tell me something, but he could only stutter and stammer and make inarticulate sounds. I could only make one word out of these stuttering attempts, and that word was 'Aristotle.' Of course he must have been half-wandering, or else I had quite misunderstood him. Just at the last, he looked more despairing than ever, and kept looking into my face so imploringly, saying 'Aristotle—Aristotle;' and not knowing what else to do, I said, 'Yes, yes, I quite understand—Aristotle—it will be all right, dear Philip.' And then he looked so wonderfully relieved, and shut his eyes and dropped into a kind of sleep, from which he never woke.'"

Mrs. Lorraine ceased reading, and looked round.

'I never could understand how it was that my saying those words could have comforted him so, but it did. I have always kept his Aristotle in remembrance of what he said; but I never could make any sense of his words, and thought I must quite have misunderstood them. I fancied afterwards that what he really wished to say was something about a will he might have made, doing more justice to Maud; but I never could see what Aristotle could have to do with it.'

'Come along!' cried Phil eagerly, springing up. 'Let us all go and search for this valuable document. Aristotle is our clue, and before an hour is over, Maud shall have her own again! Hurrah! *A bas* Belassis! Won't the old villain just curse and swear when he finds that he has betrayed the hiding-place himself!'

Maud's eyes sparkled, more with excitement at the idea of the Belassis overthrow than at any special desire for an increase of fortune. She seized Ethel by the hand, and rushed after Phil; Mrs. Lorraine followed, and Miss Marjory and Tor brought up the rear.

'This will ruin Belassis if it is found,' remarked she, as they crossed the hall.

'How so?'

'Because he's speculated with the trust-money, and lost it. He told Lewis so—told him he should be ruined if he insisted on claiming it and handing it over to Maud, as he wished to do.'

'He's a nice kind of guardian and executor!' said Tor grimly. 'Well, if this will is found, he will have to abide by the consequences of his own act.'

'And serve him right, too!' said Miss Marjory briskly. 'It is time punishment did overtake him at last.'

Already the room had been reached, and an eager search begun. Mr. Maynard's library was extensive, and not over-well arranged; but all the authors were together, and in a moment Aristotle was pounced upon, and every volume of every edition was pulled down from the shelves for inspection.

But after about five minutes of eager, rapid search, a silence and slight consternation fell upon the searchers, for it became evident that there was no will hidden away in these volumes.

'It's gone!' cried Phil dismally, 'or else it's in some of the other books. What a sell! I thought we were safe to find it. Can anybody else have been beforehand with us?'

'Not likely,' said Tor, 'as the Belassis' have failed in their attempt. Bar accident, it ought still to be here. Does anybody know if the books have been left just as they were when Mr. Maynard was alive?'

'Yes; they have not been disturbed at all,' said Mrs. Lorraine. 'They are all in their old places, as he kept them.'

'That is well,' said Tor, and strode across to where the vacant space yawned, from which the books had just been removed.

The rest crowded round him as he began a careful examination of the woodwork behind the shelves, tapping with his knuckles on every inch of exposed wood.

'There!' cried Miss Marjory suddenly; 'there's a hollow there. Try again!'

Tor did so, and the doubt became a certainty.

'There's a crack in the woodwork here, too,' he said, scanning it eagerly. 'A chisel and a hammer, and we'll see what we shall see!'

Maud darted off and quickly returned, bringing the required implements.

A little dexterous manœuvring and a square of wood fell forwards, disclosing to view a cavity into which was inserted a paper, folded square, so as just to fit the place made for its reception.

'Maud,' said Tor, turning round, 'you had better take it out. I am convinced that it is your father's last will.'

Maud's hand trembled a little as she did his bidding. In perfect silence she drew the paper out of its long-hidden place of concealment, and looked at the superscription: *'To my daughter, Maud Debenham.'*

'You open it,' she said, giving it to Tor. 'I don't feel as if I could.'

Tor obeyed. The envelope addressed to Maud contained two documents; one was a letter, the other a paper, which bore the important words, 'Last will and testament of Philip Debenham,' dated four months later than the will which had been produced by Belassis.

'Read it, Tor,' said Maud.

He obeyed. It was not a long will. It merely, as before, left all the father's property to Philip and the mother's to Maud—without any condition whatever. Mr. Twyne, the lawyer, and Mr. Maynard were appointed executors, and Mr. Maynard was made guardian to the children. Mr. Debenham seemed to have a presentiment that his hale and hearty old uncle would outlive him, as indeed had been the case. He had had an idea that he would die young, which also had verified itself. No mention whatever was made in the will of Belassis or of his son.

The letter to Maud was next read; it was a very different production from the one Mr. Belassis had brought forward.

'MY DEAR DAUGHTER,

'Four months ago I was induced by your uncle to make a will most unjust towards you, and towards your dear dead mother, my beloved wife. Why I consented to do this and to write the letter he dictated to me, need not now be explained; suffice it to say that I yielded to pressure (the nature of which you cannot understand), because I knew that it was in my power to reverse the condition which my pen had imposed upon you and upon your future.

'I have now reversed it. I have done you justice; and it is possible that you may never know the terms of the will which this one will supersede.

'My child, beware of your uncle, Alfred Belassis. Do not trust him, do not give him one particle of power over you; and above all, try not to fear him. Blind trust, followed by blind fear, has been the curse of my life. I pray that you and Philip may be delivered from a like curse.

'This fear is still master of me, bitterly though I scorn myself for it. This letter I am now writing, and the will I have just framed, must be hidden away from his sight, or I may be induced to give way to him, and do you irreparable harm. When I feel my end approaching, then and only then shall I reveal to some trusty friend the hiding-place I have selected for these precious papers.

Then and only then will you learn how much your father loved you, and how bitterly he suffered for even seeming to consent to do you so deep an injustice.

'Farewell, my dear and only daughter; think kindly and not scornfully of your weak but unhappy father.

'PHILIP DEBENHAM.'

CHAPTER XV.
THE FALL OF BELASSIS.

SOMEBODY must see Belassis about this, Phil,' said Tor, when the matter of the will had been discussed many times over, in all its bearings. 'Either you as Maud's brother, or I as her prospective husband. Which of us shall it be?'

'Oh, you,' answered Phil quickly. 'I shouldn't know what to say.'

'All right,' returned Tor. 'I'll go—and the sooner he knows his fate, the better.'

'It may be vindictive on my part,' remarked Miss Marjory, 'but I must say that I feel a savage satisfaction in picturing the overthrow of Belassis.'

Maud laughed at her look and tone.

'I'm afraid he won't be so very much overthrown, Miss Marjory. You see, he has quarrelled with Lewis, so he will not care so very much which of us has the money.'

'Perhaps he wouldn't, if there was any money to have; but as he has lost it all, he will care considerably. Lewis would hardly have sued his own father and ruined him; but your natural guardians, Maud, have no choice; and your worthy uncle will be brought to his bearings, as he richly deserves to be.'

Maud began to look grave; but Mrs. Lorraine's voice now took up the word.

'Not quite ruined—for Celia has four hundred a year settled upon her, which cannot be touched. It will keep them from actual poverty when the rest goes. I thought it a little hard once,' continued Aunt Olive, with a smile; 'for it was half what was to have been my portion—only father cut me off, and divided it between Maud and Celia, and settled it upon them. I am glad now; for I should not like Celia to be robbed of all by her bad husband, and I am so well looked after now, that I want for nothing myself.'

'Well, I'm glad that it's not absolute ruin for them,' said Tor, pulling at his moustache. 'Because the innocent always have to suffer with the guilty, and it would fall hardly on his family, richly as he deserves it all himself. Justice must be done, of course. A trustee cannot be allowed to get off, after simply robbing the legatee of her entire fortune; but it would make it harder to execute justice, if it meant absolute penury for the whole family.'

'Don't be soft, Torrington Torwood,' said Miss Marjory warningly; 'remember that Belassis made Maud's father's life a burden to him, and robbed Phil of every vestige of his inheritance. He is not worthy of your compassion. If justice never overtook the wicked, the world would come to an end faster than it is doing already.'

So after luncheon Tor started for Thornton House, with everybody's consent that he should make his own terms with Belassis.

Maud, of course, trusted him in everything, and would be satisfied with whatever arrangement he chose to make. Phil knew his friend would manage matters much better than he could do himself; and Mrs. Lorraine always felt sure that the 'first Phil,' as she often called him, could be trusted to be firm and just, and yet considerate and temperate, with all with whom he came in contact.

Perhaps Tor did not altogether relish his errand, although there was a certain satisfaction in confronting the foe, with the winning card in his hand. Nevertheless, he thought the matter would be better managed by himself than by Phil, who was likely to be too yielding one moment, and too hard the next, according as each side of the question came uppermost.

Again he found Mr. and Mrs. Belassis alone together in the study, and he fancied they looked surprised and uneasy at his appearance.

He shook hands easily and pleasantly, for in spite of their many attempts, he had never allowed himself to be drawn into a quarrel, and had always treated them with a cheerful politeness, which even the hard words given and received had never entirely overset.

'I hope your late hours have not been too much for you,' he remarked with a smile, as he took a chair opposite Mrs. Belassis. 'It is not all of us who can sit up till dawn, and not feel the effects of it afterwards.'

Dead silence followed this speech. Mr. Belassis began to grow purple. Mrs. Belassis closed her lips tightly, and looked Tor full in the face, with eyes which seemed as if they would fain read his very soul.

Had Betsy Long betrayed her?

'I do not know what you are talking about, Mr. Torwood,' she said at last.

'No? I was alluding to your visit to Ladywell last night; and hoping that your late, or rather early hours, and a two miles walk at the end of it, had not disagreed with you.'

'Ladywell!' gasped Belassis, with his usual insane attempt to escape from the inevitable. 'I haven't even been to Ladywell for weeks!'

'Then it must have been your double I saw,' answered Tor. 'A double is a nasty thing, Mr. Belassis, especially when it performs such questionable actions as yours does—stealing into people's houses at the dead of night, in order to find and destroy legal papers of great value. I should try to rid myself of such a Doppelgänger, if I were you, or you may find it lead you into trouble some day.'

The colour had all faded from Mrs. Belassis' face. She looked grey and ghastly.

'Speak out!' she said hoarsely. 'Say at once what it is you have come for.'

'I have come to thank you for a very valuable discovery which you have enabled us to make.'

'Discovery!'

'Yes; the discovery of certain papers which, but for you, would without doubt have mouldered away, unknown and unsuspected, behind the woodwork of the Ladywell library. Your nocturnal attempts to discover these same papers, and your certainty of their whereabouts, enabled others with better opportunities to make the discovery you failed to do; but it is to you, and you only, that we owe the clue. Without the information you gave us, the papers would without doubt have remained for generations in their hiding-place, which has so well concealed them for eighteen years.'

'Papers!' gasped Belassis; 'what papers?'

'Betsy Long has betrayed us!' exclaimed his wife, in the same breath.

'Not at all,' answered Tor quietly. 'Your spy, whom you so cleverly and honourably manœuvred for me to take into my service, has been loyal to you—more loyal than such creatures generally are. I am surprised that a clever woman like you, Mrs. Belassis, should stoop to use so clumsy a tool. However, such good service has been done us by all this, that it is not for me to complain. Your spy, who has been really your servant, not ours, is coming back to you this afternoon. I wish you joy of her, after the training you have thought fit to bestow upon her. No, she has not betrayed you; make yourself quite easy on that score. You betrayed yourselves by the sounds you made, and I had the pleasure and profit of seeing and hearing a good deal that passed in the library last night. It may be a satisfaction to you to hear that the papers you were so anxious about have now been found; and you are welcome to see them for yourselves any day you wish, by coming over to Ladywell.'

Mrs. Belassis was pale with rage and dismay, her husband with abject fear.

'What papers?' he gasped again.

'Philip Debenham's last will and testament—the one you were so certain he would frame, if he could, to cancel the one you wrung from him by the extraordinary influence you had obtained over him. It is all exactly as you thought. He did make another will, and hid it away at Ladywell, out of your reach. You have betrayed your own secret, and thanks to you, that will is now in our possession.'

Belassis could not speak. After a few minutes' pause his wife asked:

'And what are its terms?'

'Not any which *ought* to affect you—simply that Maud inherits her mother's fortune, principal and interest, without any condition whatever. You best know how this transfer will affect you; as I said before, apart from your paternal feeling for your son, the matter should not make the smallest difference to you.'

Belassis' face was white and rigid.

'It will only ruin me, that's all.'

'You mean to say that you have lost the money?' asked Tor coolly.

'Yes.'

'Then of course you will have to make good the loss.'

'I cannot—I have been very unlucky. I don't know how to lay my hands upon five thousand, let alone twenty, and it will come to that and more, with compound interest for all these years.'

'Well, Mr. Belassis, you understand your own affairs best, but you know the money will have to be paid.'

'I cannot pay it, I tell you!'

'You should have considered all that before you thought fit to speculate with it. Now you have no alternative in the matter. You chose to spend another person's money, and you must repay it. The whole thing is as plain as a pikestaff.'

'I can't—I tell you I can't!'

'You will soon find that you are obliged.'

'I say I can't!' cried Belassis, waxing desperate. 'You can't get blood out of a stone.'

'No, but you can get money out of an estate. You must sell your property, or transfer it, in part payment. The thing is perfectly simple.'

'What!' groaned Belassis, driven to bay; 'do you mean to tell me that my own niece would dare to turn me out of my house, to die like a dog upon the highroad, because I have been so unfortunate as to lose some money, which

I was endeavouring to turn to good account for her benefit? Do you mean to tell me that?'

'I mean to tell you,' answered Tor, repressing a strong inclination to punch the old rascal's head, 'that the law will oblige you to restore stolen property. You have squandered away Maud's inheritance in order to enrich yourself, and now you will have to take the consequences, and lose your own. You cannot play fast and loose with other people's money and not suffer for it. You cannot have your cake and eat your cake too. You chose your own course of action, and now you must abide by the results.'

'My own niece would ruin me,' moaned Belassis, 'whom I have reared like my own, and treated as a daughter. I never thought to see a day like this! I could not have believed it possible. I will *not* believe dear Maud means to be so cruel.'

'Now, Mr. Belassis, I think we have had enough of that,' said Tor firmly, and the look in his eye made Belassis quail and cease his lamentations. 'You have been the worst enemy the Debenhams have ever had or are likely to have, and you know it as well as I. You made the first Philip Debenham's life wretched by the mysterious power you obtained over him; and you deprived his son of all his inheritance; for you know as well as I, that it was thanks to you that nothing remained of the father's property. You nearly performed the same kind office for Maud; and it is by a mere accident that this second great wrong has not been successfully consummated. And yet you think it well to bring forward your claim of relationship, and hope to escape your well-merited chastisement by throwing yourself upon the mercy of the Debenhams! What mercy do you think you deserve from their hands?'

Belassis shrank into himself, and made no attempt at a reply. It was his wife who spoke first.

'What do you mean to do?'

'I have come here to ask what you mean to do.'

'I can't do anything,' groaned Belassis.

His wife gave him a look of withering contempt, and Tor said quietly:

'You will pretty soon find you have to do something, Mr. Belassis. What is the value of the property you own? You have about a couple of hundred acres, and the farm, have you not, and this house?'

'I will never give up my property!' cried Belassis fiercely. 'I will fight for it to the death!'

'Now look here, Mr. Belassis,' said Tor, in the voice which never failed to arrest attention, 'I've not got an unlimited store of patience, and if you exhaust it, you will find it all the worse for yourself. You know you will have to refund to Maud the money you chose to throw away; you understand the law better than I do, and I know that you are responsible for its restoration. And if you force us to appeal to the law, you will find yourself in a much worse position than if you come to terms quietly with us. There will be all the costs to pay, and your name will be known throughout the country as that of a dishonest trustee. I am empowered to act for Maud, and if you will arrange matters with me, you will find yourself fairly treated, and a due allowance made for the value of your property; but if you go too far, I shall simply decline to negotiate with you, and you will be forced to sell the property at what it will fetch, in order to make good the lost money. In these days, when land is a drug in the market, I leave you to judge which course is most in accordance with your own interests. It is a matter of no importance to me.'

Belassis was silenced; he began to see once again that the man before him was more than his match.

'What do you want me to do?' he asked sullenly enough.

'The only thing left for you to do—hand over the property to Maud, as payment or part payment of what you owe.'

'It is worth far more than the sum I owe.'

'That remains to be proved. We must have a valuation. We will each appoint an agent, and abide by their united decision. No doubt all that can be easily arranged later. You will be fairly dealt by, Mr. Belassis. We shall not do as we have been done by.'

'Do you mean to insult me?'

'Certainly not, unless the truth is an insult. If so, whose fault is it?'

Belassis grew a dusky red. He dared not answer Tor; but it was not pleasant to sit under his eye and hear such remarks made.

'And I suppose I shall have to go on the parish,' he remarked presently. 'My virtuous relatives will combine to drive me there.'

'Well, you can settle that point with Mrs. Belassis,' answered Tor. 'As, by a lucky chance, you really did marry her, perhaps she may consent to allow you to subsist upon her private income, which will keep her in comfort. If she does, you will get more than you deserve at her hands; but that is a question with which I have nothing to do. Mrs. Belassis, no doubt, will tell you her views on it later.'

Mrs. Belassis looked as if she meant to tell her husband her views on a variety of subjects as soon they were left in private, but all she said was:

'Have you finished the business upon which you came, Mr. Torwood?'

He rose, not at all unwilling to take his departure.

'Yes, I think you understand all that is needful now. You can make your arrangements, and communicate either with me direct, or through Mr. Twyne, as you like best. If you wish to see the late Philip Debenham's will you can do so. We will not hurry you needlessly, but remember that we wish to avoid unnecessary delays, which can only be a vexation to both parties.'

And then Tor bowed himself out, feeling that Mrs. Belassis would soon bring her husband to sense and reason, and that he could now, metaphorically speaking, wash his hands of all further dealings with them.

He had not got very far from the house before he met Maud, who had come out with the intention of waylaying him.

'Well, Tor,' she said, 'what has happened? How did they take it?'

'Pretty much as one might have expected—he like a coward and a sneak, she like a proud woman. She's no favourite of mine, Mrs. Belassis, but she has good pluck.'

'And—and—is what Miss Marjory said true? Will they be——'

'Ruined? Well, not absolutely, because Mrs. Belassis has property; but they will have to sell their place; and I should think they would prefer to retire from this part of the country altogether.'

'Oh, what a good thing!' cried Maud, with enthusiasm. 'I never could bear to think of living near Uncle and Aunt Belassis; and yet I do so like Ladywell, and should not care to go far away. You are going to live somewhere near here when—when we're married, aren't you, Tor?'

'Yes, certainly; if you wish it, little sweetheart! What should you say to Thornton House?'

'I *hate* Thornton House!' cried Maud, with energy and decision.

'You mustn't hate it, Maud; for it will soon be your own property.'

'Mine!'

'Yes; it is the only way Belassis can pay what he owes, by making over the property to you. I knew you wanted a house near Ladywell, and I have means to keep it up; so, as it seemed the only way of getting the money, it stands just as I have said.'

Maud's face brightened, and she began to smile.

'It's delightful to think of having a house of our own, Tor; and it seems to bring things so home to one, when it is really almost settled; only—only—I did so hate Thornton House when I lived there—I have always hated it!'

'It will not be Thornton House under us, Maud; we will call it Ladywell Lodge. And I'll undertake that when the present occupants have cleared out with all their belongings, and my work-people have been all through the house, decorating and furnishing, and when Miss Marjory has laid out the gardens anew, I'll undertake then that you shall not know the place again. Will that satisfy you?'

Maud looked up at him with dancing eyes.

'Of course it will! I should be satisfied with anything in the world, if you had the arranging of it!'

'It could be made a very pretty place, I have often thought, differently arranged both inside and out. Mr. and Mrs. Belassis were hardly people of taste; and their house and garden show it. You and I, Maud, will make it look very different.'

'Oh yes!' cried Maud eagerly. 'I'm sure we can. And when it is once *our* house, and Ladywell Lodge, it will never remind me one bit of that horrid old Thornton House. Oh, we shall be very, very happy! I can't understand sometimes how it is that I am so happy, and that everything has come round so delightfully! Suppose Phil had not had that sunstroke, and you had not come over! Oh dear! oh dear! I believe I should have been Mrs. Lewis Belassis by this time!'

'Horrid thought!' laughed Tor, pressing closer to him the little hand which lay upon his arm. 'You never seem to have borne me any malice for the trick I played upon you, Maud; and the unwarrantable liberties I took.'

She looked up, smiling archly.

'I hardly had time to get thoroughly angry with you, before you came and surprised me in the garden. I never had any chance of showing how dignified I can be when I am offended.'

'You certainly never did show it. I think I came off with flying colours all round. I had always looked forward with some dread to facing you all, after the revelation was made; but even that did not prove a very trying ordeal!'

'You bad boy!' said Maud; 'you took care to get your own way with me, as you do with everybody else. Why did you never confide in me, Tor; and tell me the truth, when you began to get uneasy about how things would turn out? I think you might have trusted me.'

'So I did; but I felt it would make your position a very trying one. Indeed, I think it would have been worse for both of us. And how could I tell how you would like to hear of your brother's helplessness, and see another acting in his place? It might have turned you against me!'

'Oh, Tor!' said Maud; 'you know you don't think that!'

'What?'

'That I should ever have turned against you?'

'Why should you not?'

She looked up at him and shook her head gravely.

'You can't guess, of course?'

'I was never much of a hand at guessing.'

'No? Well, then you had better remain in ignorance.'

'I don't want to remain in ignorance. I want you to tell me.'

'As if you did not know!'

'Tell me, I say.'

'I'm not sure if I will.'

'But I am—quite sure. Come, Maud; how long am I to be kept waiting?'

'You deserve to be kept all night, you tyrant! but you always do manage to get your own way. You know it is because—I love you with my whole heart!'

And with that answer Tor seemed content.

CHAPTER XVI.
THE LAST.

AND so wrong was made right, and justice overtook the evil-doer; and in a very short time the Belassis family had removed from Thornton House, taking all their goods with them, and leaving behind no pleasant regrets in the minds of others, nor even the feeling that they would be missed from the neighbourhood where they had lived so long.

No, never popular with anyone, the name of Belassis became opprobrious when the news of his conduct was noised abroad. When once the belief in his honesty had exploded, everybody had some tale to tell of his hardness or trickery or deceitfulness, and very heartily was he abused in all quarters.

'Serve him right! I hope he will feel it!' said Miss Marjory, when she heard of it. 'For I always did say you let him off far too easily, Mr. Torwood.'

'I can't hit a man when he's down,' answered Tor. 'I had too completely the whip-hand of him to use it with much force.'

'If I'd been in your place, I'd not have spared him!' cried the eager little gentlewoman. 'I'd have scared him out of his senses. He's an old villain, and doesn't deserve anybody's compassion.'

'No, he doesn't deserve any consideration at all, I quite admit,' returned Tor; 'but the fact is, he was such a pitiable and contemptible object, that one didn't care to waste words of any kind over him. You'd have felt the same if you'd been in my place, Miss Marjory. I am quite sure you would.'

'Well, well, perhaps so; but I shall always say and think that Belassis got off much more easily than he deserved—much more easily than he would have done if I'd had the handling of him.'

'Well, Miss Marjory, console yourself with the thought that his wife has had the handling of him,' answered Tor, with a smile. 'I think, if you had seen the look in her eye, you would have been content. I felt that I couldn't leave him in better hands.'

Miss Marjory laughed.

'Ah yes, there's something in that; but then I ought to have the handling of *her*; for she's almost as bad as her husband, and it's more disgraceful in her than in him, for she has good blood in her veins.'

'I should think she will be punished enough by the loss of position and wealth. She is a proud woman, and it will be a bitter pill for her to swallow, this sudden descent in the social scale. Miss Marjory, I do really think that you may make your mind easy about the Belassis family. I think their sins will be well punished.'

'Well, I hope so, I'm sure; but I shall always say you let them off too easily.'

Tor certainly behaved generously towards a fallen foe, he and Maud together; but there was no doubt as to which was the active agent in all such matters.

The valuation of the estate fell considerably short of the sum owed by Belassis to Maud; but he was not hardly dealt with when it was found that he was unable to make up the full amount. A compromise was effected; and he was even allowed to carry away into retirement the furniture, plate, glass, and china which belonged to Thornton House, and which might fairly have been claimed as compensation.

Perhaps there was less generosity in this than some people supposed, but Maud Debenham's magnanimity was greatly praised by all in the neighbourhood.

Poor Matilda and Bertha Belassis were inconsolable, and were certainly to be pitied. They came up to Ladywell several times during the 'turn-out,' and shed oceans of salt tears, and quite distorted their rather plain faces by the utter abandonment of their grief.

'Pity us, Maud! do pity us!' they would say. 'Fancy, shut up in a horrid little poky house—quite poor people we shall be—and always *with mamma*!' this seemed the climax of horror, and Maud understood it only too well.

It was a gleam of consolation when they learnt that London was to be their destination, and that their father intended going into business of some kind, to re-establish his fallen fortunes.

Maud made the best of this in her attempt to comfort them.

'You will like London ever so much: there will be such lots to see, and such heaps of people to make friends with; and when Tor and I are in town, you shall come and see us, and we will go shopping together, and to the opera and the park and everywhere. I believe you'll get to like it so much, when once you're settled, that you would never care to come back any more; and you'll wonder how it ever was that you were happy at Ladywell.'

Phil and Tor, in a good-natured way, tried with Maud to comfort the distressed damsels: and at the last they did go away somewhat cheered. Lewis was living in London, and he would probably be a well-to-do man in time; and, altogether, the rising generation of the Belassis family felt that there might be brighter days in store for them yet.

'Well, I'm glad they've gone away in better spirits, poor things!' said Maud, after the final adieu, made the very day of the journey to London. 'I am sorry for those two, because it isn't their fault; but somehow one can never feel *interested* in Matilda and Bertha.'

'Perhaps they will find some one to be interested in them in the great metropolis,' suggested Tor, smiling. 'I hope, for their sakes, that they will.'

Tor's humane wish was presently realized; and, before two years were over, Matilda and Bertha had both found husbands, infinitely to their own satisfaction.

Thornton House was at once re-named, and Ladywell Lodge became a centre for the united energy of architect, mason, and decorator. Tor's prediction, that the place would soon be changed past recognition, was amply fulfilled; and Ladywell Lodge became the envy and admiration of the neighbourhood.

Not within, alone, did the transformation scene take place. As soon as the season of the year permitted it, down came Miss Marjory from her northern home, and planting, transplanting, turfing, and changes of all descriptions went on as if by magic.

'I can't think how you know how to do it all, Miss Marjory,' cried the delighted Maud, when she came round to see what was going on. 'It's not like the same place. It will be perfectly lovely when the spring comes, and the summer. I can't think how you do it all—it's like magic!'

'If I didn't know how to lay out a garden by this time, I should be a bright specimen,' returned Miss Marjory, amused and pleased. 'I mean Mr. Torwood to have the best laid-out place in the county, because, my dear, I am very fond of him; I always feel something like a mother to him.'

Everyone agreed that Miss Marjory had achieved her object before she left; and when she did so, she carried off Maud to spend a month with her at Whitbury.

Tor had a general invitation to come whenever he pleased; and, to do justice to the 'Torwood impudence,' he was not shy in availing himself of the privilege accorded to him.

'I believe he comes more to see you than to see me, Miss Marjory,' said Maud, one day. 'I always tell him I am awfully jealous of you.'

With the twinkle in her eye, which all who knew her liked to see, Miss Marjory answered:

'Well, my dear, of course when he begins comparing you and me, it is impossible not to be aware beforehand at what conclusion he will be bound to arrive.'

Phil was married at the beginning of the new year. He and Roma made, as Miss Marjory said, a very handsome, but not a very interesting couple. They were absolutely absorbed in one another, which was very right and proper; but such people are not exciting company, and it was considered an advantage when they were safely started off for Italy, to spend their honeymoon.

Ten days later, when the bridal couple were, no one knew where, Michael Meredith was found dead in his bed one morning; and the funeral had to take place before it was possible for Phil and Roma to get back.

Tor wrote to his friend, strongly advising him to keep Roma abroad for many months, until the shock and her first grief had worn themselves out.

This he did with very successful results, and Miss Marjory was bold enough to put into words what everybody else really thought.

'Poor old man, it is well he is taken. He was a dreadful burden upon that poor girl, although she did not know it; and his sublime selfishness would have been a great trial to her and to Philip in their married life, and would have raised continual complications and difficulties. It is really a great mercy things have turned out as they have; and Roma will be a different being as Philip's wife, from what she has been as Meredith's daughter.'

The letters which reached Maud from Roma at frequent intervals, as well as those from Phil to Tor, all seemed to point to the fact that Miss Marjory's conclusion had been a correct one.

In June, Maud and Tor were married. They had seen each other so constantly that the rather long waiting had passed quickly. Tor was anxious that Ladywell Lodge should be in perfect order before he brought his young bride home to it; and it takes a long time to get a place to the state of perfection desired by an exacting man.

But at last all was ready. Mr. and Mrs. Debenham had returned, and a grand wedding from Ladywell took place, which made the excitement and talk of the place for weeks.

Miss Marjory was there, of course, in all her glory, and her present, the wedding-veil, was a marvel of antique workmanship, and almost overawed Maud by its beauty and costliness.

She tried hard to persuade her 'fairy godmother' to be first bridesmaid, but this wish was laughed to scorn.

'It's all very well for you to laugh; but I tell you there is more truth in old-fashioned sayings than you young people believe. "Three times a bridesmaid, never a bride." I've been bridesmaid twice in my life before, and do you think I'm going to throw away my chance of a husband on a slip of a girl like you?'

The wedding, however, was a brilliant success, owing, as everybody said, a great deal of its brightness to Miss Marjory's unceasing energy and unfailing flow of spirits.

The bride and bridegroom only spent a short three weeks in Switzerland, and then returned to England, and settled down in blissful tranquillity at Ladywell Lodge.

Mrs. Lorraine remained an inmate of the Manor House, where her gentle yet practical presence was of great value to the young Squire and his artist-wife, and where she was greatly beloved by all. She visited her favourite, Maud, almost daily, and would sometimes say, with tears of feeling in her eyes, that it was quite a picture and a poem to see how happy were both the children of Philip Debenham.

Certainly life seemed to flow very smoothly at Ladywell now; and the days fled by, they hardly knew how. Upon most fine evenings four people might be seen pacing the terrace or the gardens of the Manor House; Roma and Maud deep in talk, Phil and Tor arm-in-arm, sometimes talking, always smoking, ever seeming sublimely contented with themselves and their surroundings.

'This is a fine realization of all our wildest dreams—eh, Phil?' Tor would sometimes say. 'We've seen some odd passages in life, you and I; but this is a famous wind-up to it all.'

'Yes; and a much better one than it ever could have been, if you had not spent three months of your life as Philip Debenham.'

Then Tor would grin with that sense of the ridiculous which recollections of this episode always brought.

'Ah! what a time I had of it, what with one thing, and what with another! I'm glad enough I did it now; but you'll never catch me playing that game a second time, not for anyone. My recollections of some of the situations are far too vivid!'

'And what an ass I was!' Phil would say, with a fervour that showed how genuine was the sentiment. 'Just to think I could ever have been such a fool as to believe you wished to supplant me! Just to think the bother and worry and pain I gave myself believing you to be an arch-traitor and deceiver—you, mine own familiar friend!'

Four years have come and gone since then, and Ladywell Lodge is still as happy a home as ever. There is a tiny baby Phil there now, reigning supreme over all, save only the big 'papa' he adores and tries to tyrannize over with all his small might. There is, too, a prattling, laughing little Marjory, as self-willed and imperious as the 'godmother' she is continually chattering about, and who seems to hold a very high place in her infant estimation.

Miss Marjory's visits to Ladywell are a source of increasing delight and satisfaction to everybody in the place, only to be rivalled in felicity by the annual excursion of the Torwood family to the Minster House, Whitbury, where a delightful fortnight is spent year by year, in the height of the summer.

Miss Marjory is as strong and bright and imperious as ever, and quite as fully convinced that the world is rapidly coming to an end, which theory is much strengthened by the precocious utterances of her god-daughter. People say that she grows younger instead of older, and they also say that the new orchidhouse which her landlord has built for her, is one of the finest in the kingdom, and has a great deal to do with her never-failing health and happiness.

NOTE.

A case came under the author's notice some few years ago, in which a man, having sustained injury to the head, by the combined effects of a sunstroke and a fall, remained in a helpless and torpid state for above three months, and then suddenly made a steady recovery. Except for the length of time the state of torpor lasted, there is nothing, to members of the medical profession, specially remarkable in the case.